Stranger Neighbor

VIVIAN WARD CRUMP

Stranger Neighbor

This book is manufactured in the United States.

Copyright © 2016 Vivian Ward Crump

ISBN: 0-9965445-1-8
ISBN-13: 978-0-9965445-1-1

Library of Congress

FIRST EDITION paperback

Publisher:
M & K Literary Publishing
PO Box 6282
Louisville, KY 40206   *

Vivian Ward Crump
Stranger Neighbor
#2 Lingering Trilogy
A Novel

DEDICATION

In loving memory of my friend, Viola Thomas. You left fingerprints of grace on my life. You shan't be forgotten.

ACKNOWLEDGMENTS

I am thankful for all the friends and family God has given me.

To all the good people of Salyersville, Kentucky for your encouragement to finish the next book in the *Lingering Trilogy*.

To Kelci and Beth for all your editing and assistance with the writing of *Stranger Neighbor*. You are awesome!

To Chellie and Libby for your encouragement and being my sounding board when I became discouraged.

ONE

Life as she had always known it was quickly dwindling away. Sarah's soul was silently screaming this fact as she made her way to Jake's truck. She felt the tension surround her while she idly waited for Jake to finish his class. As she looked around, she marveled at the sameness of her surroundings. Everyone was doing the same as they had done the entire school year --- herself included. Students lazily made their way out of the school and into the parking lot searching for their cars and buses. The façade of normalcy flaunted a lie that everything was as it always had been and would remain the same.

Sarah sighed and propped her arms behind her, bracing on the hood of the blue Chevy truck. She stared at the activity buzzing around her. If anyone looked closely, they would see that things were indeed changing. Not only with her and Jake, but change was sparking all around them. The atmosphere of the school was changing. Everyone, including the teachers, was winding down. The days of her junior year were numbered. Before long she and Jake would be seniors. Senior year. She'd dreamed of this year her whole life. Sarah, unaware of the scowl she'd adopted, shifted her lazy stance. The fear and dread that monopolized her thoughts lately reminded her that before her senior year, she had to endure this summer – and survive.

As Sarah watched her friends and classmates making their way from school to their rides home, her eyes caught a glimpse of someone she had never seen at Salyersville High. She became aware of the deepest, clearest   blue eyes staring at her sad, frowning face.

She tried to take control of the situation by smiling and waving at the owner of those piercing eyes. She felt her inner self quiver from the intense moment that was happening as the two of them connected. The stranger smiled and waved back while strolling over to the only cherry red BMW in the student parking lot. Who was this person that had caused her to lose her breath? She knew everyone at

Salyersville High, and she was certain that she did not know this handsome stranger. She would've remembered if she'd seen him before. He was tall…at least as tall as Jake, who was six feet, four inches. He had beautiful black hair with eyes that made you look even at a distance. He didn't look as if he belonged in Salyersville. He oozed wealth from his clothes to his car; something rarely seen in the farming community of Magoffin County. He hadn't acted uppity with her. Just the opposite, he'd seemed friendly enough; he'd waved.

As she watched the stranger open the sleek door of his car, Jake came bouncing over to her. Her mind quickly forgot the guy in the cherry red BMW and turned to the light of her life. She giggled at his face and tried to be sexy as she murmured, "Hey, handsome. Can a girl get a lift?"

Jake laughed, "That might be arranged." He sauntered over to the door on the passenger side of his truck, and with a grand gesture, bowed and motioned for her to enter the Chevy.

Sarah giggled and with the same grandness made her way to the front seat of Jake's truck. "Thank you, kind sir." She reached for his face and gave him a peck on his right cheek. She could smell the distinct scent of Dulce & Gabbana aftershave, and she logged it to her memory. She'd use it later when she needed to remember things about him to get her through the lonely days of summer.

The drive home was easier than it had been lately. Sarah almost forgot the looming fate that awaited them. They both took turns controlling the conversation. They discussed everything from the upcoming four-wheeler outing to Sarah's observation of the new boy at school.

Jake hadn't seen the owner of the red BMW, but he had definitely seen the car. "Did you see that brand new BMW sitting in the parking lot today? I've wondered all day about who could afford a car like that in Salyersville." Sarah didn't feel the need to answer Jake. He was talking to himself as much as he was speaking to her. "I mean; how can any kid afford to drive a car that expensive to school --- especially here in Salyersville?"

"I've been wondering the same thing," Sarah smiled. Just for a moment, she hesitated before telling

Jake she'd met the owner of the car. She wasn't sure why she was keeping quiet about the new guy she'd seen in the parking lot; it wasn't like anything had happened that she couldn't talk about with Jake.

After struggling with her inner self for a moment she decided to tell Jake about the encounter with the new boy. "Although," she paused, "I did see the owner today while I waited for you to finish your class." She glanced at Jake knowing he would be biting at the bit wanting to know more. She giggled at his complete attention with obvious anticipation of what she knew, "You can tell he isn't from around here. He had on dress pants and walked to his car all stiff like and didn't try to speak with anyone. He could've been one of the teachers if he didn't look as young as us."

Sarah made sure not to mention how cute he was and how his eyes just pulled her toward him. She didn't see the need to tell Jake all of what had occurred in the parking lot earlier. Jake didn't know that she had left out parts of the description, so why should she reveal how she had felt about this mysterious new guy?

Just as Jake was asking about his name, the red BMW raced past them. They had turned up Elk Creek Road that led to Buffalo Creek when the BMW passed them. Jake and Sarah both looked at each other with wide eyes. Jake mumbled, "What the ..." he didn't need to finish; Sarah knew what he was thinking. What was going on? Who was this person flying up their road in this flashy red BMW?

Just as Sarah wrapped her brain around the scene of a BMW with a teenager at the wheel, they saw the red car moving along in front of them toward Buffalo Creek. "I can't believe this. What on earth is he doing on Buffalo Creek?" Neither, Jake nor Sarah could believe their eyes. Sarah cried, "What explanation could there possibly be for this guy to be in Salyersville? Who comes to the foothills of the Appalachian Mountains unless your family is here.

TWO

Jake turned his truck into Sarah's driveway, and they sat for a moment without speaking. Finally, Sarah asked the unanswered question again. "Who is that stranger and why on earth is he driving up Buffalo Creek?"

Jake turned toward Sarah shaking his head in disbelief, "I can't imagine any reason for him to be in our town let alone on Buffalo Creek." He stared after the long gone BMW. "How did he find his way here? We know everybody on this creek, and I've never heard of anyone having rich relatives." As if investigating the mystery of what had just happened, Jake smiled, "Are you holding back secrets of long-lost wealthy aunts and uncles?"

Sarah giggled, "No rich uncles or aunts that I know of; don't know if Mom and Dad are keeping estranged, rich relatives a secret." She looked at Jake, "How about you, any of your family on the high end of the money tree?"

Jake laughed, "I'm pretty sure if I had rich family I'd know about it. They'd definitely be on my favorite family members list."

Sarah became solemn for a few minutes thinking about the few times Jake and she still had to kid around. In only a few short weeks their afternoons together would be gone until another season. She looked deep into his dark eyes and saw that he knew her pain. It was obvious that his pain matched her own. Usually, she didn't mention the upcoming summer, but she allowed her thoughts to escape her lips, "Oh, Jake." That was all she said --- nothing else --- there was no need or reason to go on.

Jake didn't speak. He held her close for what could have been minutes or an hour. They were lost in their thoughts until Sarah's mom arrived from her visit to one of the local farms. Sarah was proud of her mom. She was the community veterinarian and worked in all the surrounding counties as well as Magoffin County.

Sarah smiled as her mom sprang out of the truck and greeted them. "Hey, guys. How was school?" Not waiting for an answer she asked, "Are you ready for a break? Just think, next year is the big senior year."

Jake nodded, "I know. It doesn't seem possible that we're almost finished with high school." He looked at Sarah, "Seniors." He allowed the word to roll over his tongue. "We'll soon rule the halls of Salyersville High."

Sarah laughed. He knew just how to get her away from being depressed. She knew that Jake didn't care about being the Big Man on Campus. She also knew her mother was trying to get them to see past the next few months. To some extent, her mother's strategy was working. Sarah was trying to think in the future --- past the summer. It worked for a while then the reality of the nearing summer would invade her thoughts. The acknowledgment of the impending loneliness would suffocate her until she made herself find someone (anyone) to help take her mind off of the dismal challenge of being alone for the summer.

She and her mother had discussed her helping with her mom's veterinary practice. She always learned so much when she got to observe her mother in action. She couldn't wait until she got to practice alongside her in the field. Working with her mom was the one positive thing this summer promised, and she was going to hold on to that bit of joy as a reminder of the small hope for fun this summer.

In the meantime, she had her other half-of-life with her, and she was going to enjoy him. "Jake, can you stay for dinner?" She turned toward her mom and raised her eyebrow as if asking "okay?" Her mom nodded her agreement, and they both turned to Jake for an answer.

Jake grinned and laughed, "Thought you'd never ask. I'll call Mom first, but I'm pretty sure she'll be good with it. Thanks, Mrs. Arnett." He pulled out his phone and a few minutes later, he and Sarah were walking toward the barn to check on Heine, Sarah's new horse.

Joyce watched as Sarah strolled across the barn lot, hand in hand with Jake. Joyce shook her head because she knew that eight weeks were going to be an eternity for her daughter.

During dinner, Sarah's dad announced that the farm at the head of the creek had sold. "Down at

Mark's Feed Store today I found out that the old Gamble Farm was finally sold, after all these years. I'm not sure who bought it or how they got through the red tape and all the title-holders to actually purchase the property. I guess no one would even know it sold if a man with a Connecticut license plate hadn't stopped in at The Feed Store wanting to know where the best place was to hire a cleaning crew. I guess there's a lot that needs to be cleaned up around there since it's been vacant all these years."

"Didn't Mark find out anything about him? He should have asked questions. We need to know about our new neighbors," Joyce declared. She looked around the table at her husband, Sarah, and Jake for affirmation. Everyone agreed that it would be nice to know what was happening up the road. Joyce directed her attention toward Jake. Maybe his parents had heard something. "Do Alma and Morris know anything about this?"

Jake shook his head showing his puzzled reaction to the news. "I don't think they've heard anything yet. I haven't heard them talking about it, so I'm fairly sure they don't know." After dinner, Sarah and Jake didn't go anywhere. They tried to watch CSI on TV, but neither could keep their minds on the plot.

Sarah snuggled as close as she dared and Jake held on just as tightly. They didn't talk about anything. They just sat and held each other, trying to absorb the other's presence. At 10 o'clock Joyce came in to announce that it was a school night, and they had to say goodnight. Jake kissed his girlfriend and whispered, "Good night until morning." Then he was gone.

Usually, this didn't bother Sarah, but tonight she felt an emptiness in the house when the door closed, and he wasn't there anymore. She scolded herself. She had to stop this sad, pathetic mood. Jake wasn't gone and would not be gone for two more weeks, and she didn't want to bring on the pain that was sure to come soon enough. She stopped to turn off the light switch and stretched as if she were stretching off the bad mood that loomed over her. She headed to bed looking forward to seeing Jake waiting to take her to school in the morning.

THREE

The next morning Sarah made her way down the walkway eager to see her boyfriend who was waiting for her in his old blue Chevy truck. Reaching the truck, she bounced up into the passenger's seat and leaned over to get her good morning kiss. Jake did not disappoint her. Their morning kiss was beginning to linger longer and longer as their time together got shorter and shorter. She would have stayed with her lips tangled with Jake's for the entire day had he not pulled away. He chuckled. "Gosh, girl, you're in a loving mood this morning, not that I'm complaining." He flashed a smile at her as he caressed her hair.

She returned his smile, but it didn't reach her eyes. She loved this boy sitting beside her. She had known and loved him her whole life. They lived on adjoining farms, and their parents had put them together from the time they were babies. They had easily transitioned from best friends to boyfriend and girlfriend.

Sarah refused to allow the all too familiar gloom to steal the best part of her day. She considered this time of the day as their time away from everything going on around them. They used the time to concentrate on each other and to enjoy the drive. Today, enjoying each other, while ignoring everything, would be hard. The thing that was bothering Sarah the most was sitting next to her. She tried not to think of Jake's leaving, but as much as she wanted to enjoy their last days, seeing his cute face brought a stabbing reminder of his impending absence. He would be leaving soon.

They had discussed his leaving when he received his acceptance to the Young Male Appalachian Academic Achievement Program from the University of Kentucky. They both had planned for the upcoming separation through the winter and spring. Sarah was bracing herself for her lonely summer while Jake got more excited every day for his good fortune of studying with the Medical College at the University.

Sarah and Jake both wanted to attend the

University of Kentucky. Jake wanted to become a doctor, and she hoped to follow her mother's footsteps and become a veterinarian. She just had to make it through the lonely weeks of summer and life would be back on track.

Her friend Cassie had her mind set on attending the University of Louisville and so, of course, her boyfriend, Josh would follow her. And since Louisville was a short distance from Lexington, she was confident that the four of them would be visiting each other often. She smiled at her planning of their lives a whole year away. They still had senior year to enjoy. There would be time later to make plans for their futures.

As summer came speeding up on them, thinking about her loneliness was almost more than Sarah could bear. Summer was her favorite time of the year, but this year's season was going to be miserable. She couldn't even count on Cassie, her best friend, to help see her through her sadness. Cassie had announced last week that she would be going back to Louisville to visit her dad and new baby sister for a month this summer.

This announcement was a big deal. It was only last year that Cassie was struggling with her father's drug addiction. She had come a long way in dealing with the breakup of her family since she first moved to Howard Farm. Sarah had been happy for Cassie when she told their group she was going to spend time with her father. Although, she couldn't help but feel sorry for herself because of her imminent loneliness. What would she do alone in Salyersville, the entire summer?

Jake turned away from Sarah, concentrating on putting the truck in gear and heading onto the road going toward Salyersville and school. He had not said anything about her sad face although he had noticed. He was sure that once summer was here, and Sarah was in a routine, she would be okay. He hated that he would not be allowed to call her for two whole months. The YMAAAP strictly forbid students from calling home. He would only be allowed one Sunday evening for visitors, and that was only for his parents. Even the one visit wouldn't happen until midway through the program. He didn't mind at all except for Sarah. He would miss her so much, but this was an opportunity he could not pass up. This summer was the beginning of his journey to becoming a doctor and someday, when this summer was just a memory, he and Sarah would smile at their sadness.

At least that's what his mom had said when he'd asked her to make sure Sarah was okay during the summer. She'd promised to keep Sarah busy while Jake was away.

Alma could see the stress her son was experiencing because of his upcoming opportunity. "Jake you need to look forward to the neighborhood picnic you guys will enjoy when you get back home." Jake tried to smile and nod.

He hadn't forgotten, but it would be many days and weeks before the picnic came around. This year, Jake's family had offered up their east pasture for the picnic since they had moved their livestock to the woods behind the barns leaving a large field between their home and the barns. Jake felt a touch of sadness when his mom had told him about their decision to host the picnic this year; even though he knew his summer would hold some amazing experiences --- at least he hoped. He was aware that all the planning and preparing for the picnic would be finished before he returned home. At least he would get home in time to enjoy the event.

This morning both Sarah and Jake were more quiet than usual. It was evident that both of them were deep in thought about this summer. He could see that Sarah was trying hard not to show her emotions. She sat looking out the window with a smile pasted on her lips. He had known this girl his whole life, and he knew she was hiding behind her smile. He guessed he also was hiding with his upbeat chatter and jokes. It was hard to face the fact that the two of them would not be seeing each other for so long. They hadn't been separated this long their entire lives.

When he and his mom discussed how hard it was to be leaving not only his girlfriend but also his best friend for two whole months without any contact, she remarked that it would be good for them. In her words, this summer would be a test of how devoted they are to each other. If they made it through the summer, and the different experiences each would surely have and in the end feel the same closeness to each other, they would know the bond they felt was real. And, if their closeness wasn't there after their separation this summer, it would be better to know

now than to wait until down the road when they had both invested so much of their lives with each other. He understood what his mom was saying—they had been joined as a couple their whole lives.

Jake was sure that both of their families wondered if they were close because it was easy for the two of them to be together or if it was truly a bond of love that drew them to each other. He knew in his heart that Sarah was a love that only happens once, and he was sure that she felt the same. The families only wanted the best for the two of them, and if it worked out, they would be ecstatic about their union.

Their families were good friends. His father and Sarah's father were best friends, often helping each other out on their farms. Jake's dad, Morris Collins, moved to Buffalo Creek when he married Jake's mom, Alma. Alma's family had owned the Gullett farm for several generations. Dan, Sarah's dad, always kidded Morris about being a transplant. Since Dan had always lived in Magoffin County, he felt he had bragging rights to being a native of Buffalo Creek. Still, Sarah's mom often reminded her husband that he was a city boy from the great town of Salyersville. This fact brought giggles from anyone listening since Salyersville's population was only around ten thousand people, and that included the people living out in the county seat, like the Collin's and the Arnett's.

Just like Alma, Sarah's mom, Joyce had lived on her family farm her whole life except for the eight years when she moved away to attend college. She had never had any doubts about coming home to raise her family on the farm.

Alma was about four years younger than Joyce. Even though they had been neighbors during their childhood, they had not been close until they both began raising their families on the farms. Now they were best friends, and their families were close, helping with work when each other's farms needed significant attention.

Jake grabbed his girlfriend's hand as he stopped his pickup in front of Salyersville High. He pulled her to him for one last kiss before going to class. Sarah's smile became genuine when their lips parted, and she pushed him away and jumped out of the truck racing to the driver's side. Jake had made his way out of the truck and locked the door by the time she'd run to his side. He turned to lock his arms around her and kissed her on top of her head as if she were a little sister, not chancing another lingering kiss. If they kissed again, neither would want to go to class. He dropped his arms, reached for her hand, and they ran to the entrance of the building racing to their separate classes.

Sarah could not wait until lunch. She wanted to meet up with Cassie and Josh and their other friends. Their group was close, and she was hopeful that a few of the gang staying in Salyersville during summer vacation would help keep her busy while Jake was away.

As she walked into the cafeteria, she saw the group of friends in their usual spot. Cassie and Josh were sitting to one side of the table while Seth and Will were fooling around telling jokes on each other, making everyone laugh. Jake sat on the other end of the table with an empty seat for her. She smiled and made her way to his side. She gave him a quick peck on the lips and smiled at Cassie. She was so glad her friend had moved to Magoffin from Louisville.

Sarah had never had a best friend, except for Jake, so having a girl best friend had been awesome this past year. The thought brought a fleeting sadness to her because Cassie would be gone this summer too. Sarah brightened when she remembered that unlike Jake and her, Cassie and she could keep in touch, and she would come home in a month.

"Hey, guys," Sarah dropped her books on the table and looked over at Cassie.

"Hey, Sarah," Cassie pouted, "It's been a long morning. I am so ready for this school year to be over. I didn't think this morning would ever end."

Sarah nodded in agreement although she did not feel the same sentiment as Cassie. She knew that her summer would mean long lonely days of working on the farm and her mom's clinic with only senior citizens to keep her company. What a bummer. She remembered her promise to Cassie that she would help her mom out on their farm while Cassie was away. "Cassie, did you ask your mom what she wanted me to do while you are away?"

Cassie smiled at her friend, "We talked about it.

Sarah, Mom is so happy you'll be visiting and helping with the farm chores. I can't thank you enough."

Sarah smiled back at her friend, "I am more than happy to help out. Does she have a list of chores for me yet?"

"No, I think she is just happy someone will be there to keep her company while I'm in Louisville. You won't mind being in the house, will you? I would totally understand if you don't want to hang around with the stuff that happens sometimes." Cassie searched Sarah's face for an answer.

Both girls flashed back to the last year when Cassie had almost moved from her great-grandparents' home because of unexplained occurrences that happened in the house and on the farm. Sarah remembered Cassie's mom being scared for her safety and nearly moving Cassie and her back to Louisville. Fortunately, the occurrences settled down, so the Wards felt safe to stay in the house again. Later, Cassie revealed to Sarah that things still occurred in the home but not nearly as severe as when they first moved into the place.

Sarah didn't care that Cassie's house was full of paranormal incidents. She had been at the Howard Farm plenty of times and had never experienced anything strange. Still, Cassie was very secretive about her house. Only Josh's family, Sarah, and Cassie's mom's friend Mark knew about the happenings at the Ward's home. Sarah reassured her friend she did not mind going to her home and would find visiting her mom as helpful for her loneliness as Cassie's mom's loneliness.

As they ate their lunch, everyone was talking about their upcoming summer plans. It seemed that everyone had plans except Sarah. She sat quietly and listened to the excitement around the table. Jake was aware of his girlfriend's mood and linked her hand with his, giving it a squeeze and releasing only slightly, keeping her securely close to him. She squeezed back, and her blue eyes brightened.

Jake absentmindedly tangled his free hand into Sarah's long red hair and effortlessly steered the conversation from their summer plans to discussing the new kid who was showing up everywhere. So far no one had spoken to him or even been in a class with him. The only thing anyone knew about him was that he drove an expensive BMW. Jake shared the story about the day before when he and Sarah had seen him driving up Buffalo Creek and how Dan, Sarah's dad had discovered the old Gamble Farm was sold. "I wonder if Mr. BMW and the farm have anything in common?"

Sarah wondered the same thing, ever since her dad told them about the farm being sold. That farm had been for sale as long as she could remember. Her mother had told her about the owners of the farm. It had belonged to an old couple, Jed and Susan Gamble. Their kids, all twelve of them, had moved away years ago, and the two had lived on their farm alone. When they passed away, the heirs to the estate refused to settle on the division of the assets from the farm, and it had lain in ruin for these many years.

Sometimes Sarah and her friends rode their four-wheelers to the Gamble Farm to picnic or on occasions just to hang out. It was perfect except for an occasional unexplainable incident. The farm sat at the end of the creek, nestled up against the ridge that divided Buffalo Creek from Lick Creek. The place was vacant, but things kept moving on them when they were there. Sarah had noticed that their horses were always on edge when they rode them up to the farm for picnics. But they always went back. They loved the peaceful, quiet and isolation from the outside world that the farm offered. And the farm was their trail to Cassie and Josh's farms.

The gang would miss going to the farm they had claimed for their own. Sarah had secretly dreamed of owning Gamble Farm someday and raising a family there with Jake. There would be lots of work to get it back in shape, but that would be part of the fun when the time came. Now that dream was fleeting away.

Lunch was soon over, and they all went their separate ways promising to meet up tomorrow for their four-wheeler ride and picnic. Sarah loved these outings with her friends. They made plans to meet at the foot of the hill on Cassie's farm, near a large elm tree that sat next to a small stream. The tree looked peaceful, but as Cassie and others would tell you, strange things happened around this tree and stream. So far, neither she or her friends had experienced anything; although, Cassie confided to her that she had been scared while sitting under the tree when she first moved onto the farm.

She told Sarah that she felt the presence of someone breathing on her neck while she was resting under the tree. After the one incident, nothing else had happened. Cassie was comfortable with the area now so they agreed the tree would be their regular meeting spot since it was convenient for everyone.

After school, Sarah rushed to Jake's truck. She was ready for the weekend to begin. They had exactly two weekends left, and she was going to savor each second of them. She made her way to the truck to find she had beat Jake out of the building. She lazily leaned against the truck and watched the parking lot come alive with teenagers.

As she looked on, she noticed the red BMW parked only two spaces away from Jake's blue Chevy truck. While she was admiring the BMW, she neglected to see the owner coming toward her and his car. She moved closer to the car, checking out the interior through the driver's side window when she heard a "hum-hum." Sarah jumped away from the window.

Embarrassed, she looked into the new student's eyes. His gaze was just as piercing as the first time she had seen him walking through the parking lot. She couldn't help but notice the crystal clear blue of his eyes as he quizzically looked down at her. She could feel her face blushing. She knew that her freckles were popping from under the red of her face and that knowledge made her blush more. As she gained her composure, she stuttered, "I was just admiring your car. It's something else--Very nice. We don't have many of those parked in the student parking lot." She laughed lamely at her attempt of casual conversation. She decided it was time to shut her mouth before she stuck her foot even farther down it. She waited for him to speak. He didn't.

Sarah found herself scrambling for words once again. This boy made her nervous, and that was saying something. Usually, she was relaxed with everyone she met. But, not this time. Surely it was because as of yet she hadn't got him to speak. She finally held her hand out and stated, "Hi, I'm Sarah Arnett. I live down the road from the old Gamble Farm. Isn't that your new home?"

Finally, the dark, crystal blue eyes crinkled on the sides, and a smile reached down to his mouth. At that moment, Sarah's only thought consisted of the fact that it was a perfect mouth. He held his hand out to take Sarah's and replied, "Hi, Samuel Lazra. I guess I'm your new neighbor. I thought I recognized you in that truck yesterday when I was going back to the farm after school."

He recognized me from the parking lot, and he noticed me from the truck. Wow, Sarah thought. She struggled to bring herself back to the present and remarked, "Yes, Jake and I thought that was you, but we wondered why you were visiting our little creek. We had no idea that your family had bought the Gamble Farm. It's one of my favorite places on Buffalo Creek."

"Yes, it's a secluded and beautiful spot. I think once we finish reclaiming, it will be a beautiful farm." He smiled at Sarah. She smiled back. Oddly, the conversation was both intense and easy for Sarah.

"So, what brought your family to the small town of Salyersville? I don't think I've heard of any Lazra's that are from here." She thought this was a natural progression of the conversation, but she must have said something wrong because Samuel's face became cloudy. He immediately lost his smile.

"I have to go. My mom expects me home by 4 o'clock. Nice meeting you Sarah Arnett." He opened his car door and slid in before Sarah had a chance to respond. She watched as he sped away. Once he was gone, she realized that he had not told her anything about himself that she didn't already know. What a strange meeting.

She absently walked back to Jake's truck, and while she was still marveling over the conversation she'd just had with Samuel Lazra, Jake sauntered over to her. "Hey, pretty lady what's wrong? You look like you're troubled about something."

Sarah shook her head of all thoughts of the previous conversation with Samuel and focused on her handsome boyfriend standing in front of her. "Hey back at you, handsome! I'm not troubled. I guess I'm puzzled about the conversation I had with the new guy a few minutes ago."

Jake's face became serious. "What did you find

out that has made you so serious?" He stared at Sarah expectantly. He couldn't imagine what this boy had said to Sarah that had her in such a state. "Where did you meet him?"

Sarah tried shaking her mood and replied, "His car was parked over there, and I guess he caught me checking it out. I was looking in the window and admiring the dash when he came over." She smiled at her nosiness.

Jake's face lost its easiness, "What did he say to you, Sarah? Was he rude to you? I'll hunt him down."

Sarah grabbed Jake's arm. "Whoa, big boy! He was very polite and courteous during the whole conversation. He didn't say anything about my snooping. He seemed entertained by my curious examination of his car."

Jake settled and his curiosity took the place of protection mode. "Tell me what was said."

Sarah shrugged, "Not much. He said his name was Samuel Lazra and that his family did buy the Gamble Farm. They're fixing it up. I think he used the word 'reclaiming.' When I asked why his family had moved to Salyersville, he shut down and left quickly. I guess that's what left me in such a mood. He seemed friendly and kind yet he was very secretive about his family."

"I'm going to miss going up to Gamble Farm and spending the day lying under that big weeping willow tree in the yard." She looked sadly over at Jake wanting him to agree with her. She wasn't disappointed. Jake was nodding his head remembering their times spent on the farm.

He took a moment as if weighing what he should say next and finally said, "I'll miss going up there too."

Their mood brought back Sarah's constant impending sadness that loomed closer each day. "Jake, I am so going to miss you this summer." There, she said it. Now it was out in the open. No more pretending that everything was okay. It was NOT okay. Jake would be gone out of her life for eight whole weeks, and that was not okay on any terms. Although; Sarah understood Jake's excitement about the University of Kentucky summer program. She was excited for him and wouldn't take this opportunity away from him for anything but still--her impending loneliness was indescribable. She looked into Jake's eyes and whispered, "Don't forget who loves you back here and who wants you to come back home as my Jake."

Jake's look matched Sarah's, and he whispered back, "Not a chance that I will forget my girl. You remember that I will be thinking and missing you each and every day I'm gone." He pulled her close and hugged as hard as he dared without hurting her. It was as if he wanted to make his imprint of the two of them together.

Suddenly he pushed her an arm's length away from him, and Sarah saw his blue eyes dancing. Jake shouted, "I've got it. Let's make a designated time that the two of us will stop what we are doing and think of each other. It needs to be the same time every day. What time do you think will work?"

Sarah giggled. She liked this idea. She would feel connected to Jake in some weird way. "Okay, let's say at 4 o'clock each day we will stop whatever we are doing and think of each other. Send thoughts of love to each other through our psychic connection."

"Four o'clock it is. Let's set an alarm on our phones so we won't forget and at 4 o'clock each day we'll think about our love for each other. Kind of like telepathy stuff." He smiled, satisfied with himself for thinking of such a grand idea.

Sarah gave him one last squeeze before jumping into the passenger's side of the blue Chevy. Her heart felt lighter after Jake's brilliant idea, and her face showed the glow that she had lost the last few weeks. Her better mood was not lost on Jake. He felt a little lighter himself. He hated seeing Sarah miserable about anything let alone the fact that he was the cause of her misery. It was too much for him. But he had been able to make her feel better for the time being, and he was going to take advantage. He jumped into the truck and headed out of town toward Buffalo Creek and the Arnett's barn. "Let's get Heine out and work him, if you want."

Sarah became excited. "Yes, please." She had wanted to work her new horse for a few days. They had already become good friends, but Sarah knew she needed to have Jake to help her with getting her new horse ready for riding. She was good, but Jake was known to be one of the best with horses. Sarah called him the Horse Whisperer. He had helped her break more than one horse to ride. She loved the horses on the farm. Often the gang still rode in the hills behind the barn and pastures. It was true that four-wheeling had taken some of their horse riding time, but once in a while, they would ride their horses up the ridge and around the hill to Cassie's farm.

Sarah's dad had found Heine while looking at some cattle to buy during a trip to a farm in neighboring Morgan County. He had brought Heine home and called Sarah out of the house to help with getting the cattle into the barn stalls. When Sarah got close to the truck with the trailer of livestock, she noticed the prettiest black horse with white markings on his face. She fell in love the moment she saw him. Her dad knew she would. He loved being able to tell her that Heine was hers if she took care of him and trained him right. She promised to take care of him the way a fine horse like Heine deserved. She hugged her dad with a squeal to seal the deal.

She made sure his food and water troughs were full. She brushed him every evening and talked with him. Heine was very receptive and seemed to perk up when Sarah entered the barn. Today was no different. When Jake and Sarah led Heine from his stall, he seemed as excited as Sarah. Jake was amazed at the bond the two had already formed.

Watching the two of them prance around the pasture was like a picture. Heine would do anything that Sarah asked the horse to do. Sarah's face was flushed with excitement while she rode atop of the magnificent animal. Each time she rode him she learned just how good at riding he was. She was so happy to have him. He would help her get through this summer without Jake. She would spend her days with Heine. She smiled. That is what she would do--ride her faithful horse all day long. Thinking of being alone without Jake all summer still made her sad, but then she thought of Heine and the fun he would bring her while riding.

After they had finished working with Heine, he ate and enjoyed his rub down. Then they fed the rest of the livestock in the barn and cleaned the horses' stalls. Once the chores were finished, Jake announced he was starved. Sarah agreed that she was hungry although not starved. Since their time together was short, their parents had slacked on the time limit that they could spend together. Jake stayed for dinner almost every night now. They walked back to the house and when they entered they could smell the delicious aroma of dinner. Jake sniffed. "I think we're having steak and potatoes with a side salad. I hope your mom stopped in town for those rolls we like so much."

Sarah laughed, "You mean you like them so much, right?'"

Jake gave her a sideways glance and pursed his lips. "Exactly what are you trying to say?" They both burst out with a laugh and grabbed each other's hands while slowly walking up the path to the house.

When they entered the kitchen, the smell of steak grilling was overwhelming. "If I hadn't already been starved, that smell would have brought my taste buds to attention. Man, that smells delicious." Jake smacked his lips.

When Joyce came into the kitchen, she found the two giggling as usual. "Have a nice day?" Without waiting for an answer, she rolled off the menu for the evening. She watched as Jake became engrossed with the words she was saying. She smiled at his reaction. Of course, he was overplaying it just a smidge, but she loved that he enjoyed her food so much.

"Dinner will be served in about half an hour." She shooed them out of the kitchen while guiding them toward the TV room with her hands. She left them alone to do whatever they did in the TV room, which was to play video games, watch Ellen on TV or whatever. As she resumed cooking dinner, they both shouted, "Thank you!" She waved a dismissal and turned the sizzling steaks.

Sarah and Jake moved to the TV room and sank onto the couch next to each other. They talked about the next day's four-wheeling date they had with the gang. Sarah was looking forward to the day. Their best friends would all be together for one last time before the summer began. Sarah felt a strange intuition that this season would bring them all back changed in the fall. She shrugged off the feeling before Jake saw the dark cloud that settled on her face.

But Jake did notice. He thought she was

thinking about his leaving and so decided to leave it alone and talk about happier things. "I am so ready to get out on the ridge tomorrow. I was talking about the run with Seth, and he thinks he might bring Isabelle, that girl from Johnson County he's been seeing."

"Good, I liked her when she was with him during the movies. Cassie and I could use some good girl company while you little boys go horsing around!" she laughed.

Jake pulled his innocent yet guilty as sin face. It worked. Sarah was in a much better mood.

Sarah was honest. She wanted the boys to find girlfriends who fit into their group without the drama that Josh's girlfriend before Cassie had brought to the friends. Kari had been too much for Josh and the rest of them. They tolerated her because of Josh, but she was always putting them down as if she was better than they were. When Cassie had moved to town, and it was obvious that Josh was smitten. Kari tried to get Josh back, but her scheming didn't work. Sarah was happy because Cassie had become her best friend.

Isabelle seemed kind. Sarah hoped she came

tomorrow and that Seth and Isabelle became as happy as Cassie and Josh. It was entertaining to watch new love.

She and Jake didn't go through the "new phase" in their relationship. They had known each other since they were babies, and their connection had always been there. As far back as Sarah could remember, she remembered feeling close to this handsome boy sitting beside her.

And he was handsome. She wasn't so comfortable with their relationship that she didn't notice how girls flirted with him right in front of her. Jake had the prettiest dark blue eyes and lips that were full and showed just enough of his white teeth when he smiled. He was six feet and four inches tall, towering over Sarah's five feet, six inches. He had worked on the farm his whole life so that his muscles were hard and firm. His shoulders were broad and strong. Yep, she had a keeper. She grabbed his face and gave him a smack on his lips. He stopped talking and looked at her.

"What was that for?" He pretended to be shocked. "You need to give a fella a little warning. I can't prepare to give my best when it's on the fly like that." He smiled as he came over for another. "Now that I'm aware let's try again." Sarah didn't resist but gave in to his lips and marveled at their gentle caress on her own.

Time stood still, and they forgot about dinner until they heard Sarah's dad in the doorway, "Hum-hum. Dinner is waiting." They both pulled apart shyly and followed her father to the table. Jake dived in for a large slab of rib eye, while taking three rolls to start his feast. He looked up with baked potato hanging on his fork and noticed everyone staring at him. He smiled, "I didn't get time to have much lunch today. We were planning our four-wheeler ride for tomorrow, and it was time for class before I realized…and I love a good steak." They all laughed, including Jake.

FOUR

Around 8 o'clock the next morning Jake came roaring to a stop in front of Sarah's house. Eagar to spend every minute of the day with Jake and their friends, Sarah wasn't her usual slow self. She was ready and waiting for Jake when he drove up the driveway. She raced out the door yelling her goodbyes as she left.

Sarah gave Jake a kiss, jumped on the back of the four-wheeler, and off they went. She smiled as she felt the cool morning air caress her face. She gripped tightly around Jake's waist as they began climbing the hill behind the barn. Once up the hill, they began their journey around the ridge. It was only minutes until they heard two four-wheelers coming toward them. Seth and Isabelle were on one, and their friends Cameron and Carol Ann were on the other. They nodded to each other, not attempting to talk over the roar of the four-wheeler engines. Jake and Sarah moved to the front and led the way toward Cassie's farm. The sun was shining and getting warmer as they moved around the ridge. Sarah relaxed against Jake's back enjoying the moment.

She was lost in the feeling of the wind and sun on her face when Jake abruptly stopped the four-wheeler. The roar of the other two four-wheelers gradually came to a halt also. When Sarah pulled herself away from Jake's back to check out what was going on, she saw that they had made it to the Gamble Farm. She had forgotten about Samuel's family buying the place. It was hard not to notice that bit of information now. There were several men placed at the boundaries of the land.

Nothing else looked different about the land-- just several men in dark suits scattered along the boundary line of the farm. What reason could these men have for standing around the property, as if guarding the land? Or was that exactly what they were doing? By all appearances, they looked like posted guards; they only lacked large rifles strapped to their shoulders. Sarah found herself wondering if they did have guns, but kept them out of sight.

Seth and Cameron pulled their four-wheelers up next to the side of Jake's. Seth asked not to anyone in particular, "What is going on down there?"

Jake answered mostly to himself, "That's what I was wondering. What on earth is going on in this little holler?" He shook himself, "Let's go down the ridge and back up the hill on the other side of the property; we don't want to interfere with whatever this is."

Just as they started their engines, one of the men noticed them. Sarah watched as he became alert and yelled to his partner, then, nodded toward them. Sarah felt her heart throbbing in her throat. She was scared, and she wasn't sure why. Finally, she got her senses back and decided to act calm and neighborly. She waved at the men in suits as if their being in this holler on Buffalo Creek was as natural as seeing deer roaming around. One of the men caught her eyes and time stood still as they stared at each other. She watched as the harsh, stern look on his face broke into a stiff smile, and he raised his hand to her. As she looked at his face, she found his eyes loathing at her. She felt uneasy and scared. She put her lips next to Jake's ear, "Can we hurry up and get out of here, Jake?"

Jake nodded and began speeding toward the trail leading down the ridge and away from their beautiful Gamble Farm. Sadness set in as Sarah realized that they would not be having any more picnics there. But she was determined not to let this incident ruin her good mood. After a few minutes thinking about the farm she focused on the boy in front of her and the wind on her face. She tightened her grip around his waist, not because they were climbing a steep hill, but because she was so glad to be riding with him. The wind brought his distinct aroma back to her, and she breathed him in and smiled. She was going to be Scarlett from "Gone With The Wind" and think about Gamble Farm tomorrow.

As they found their way to the clearing on the Howard's farm, Sarah saw another four-wheeler coming toward them. She was anxious to ask her friends if they had seen any of the men on the other side of Gamble Farm. Will and Lindsey had come from the north side and met up with them where the Howard Farm began. She would wait until they stopped to join Cassie and Josh to question them.

The four-wheelers began their descent to the

valley at the bottom of the mountain where Cassie and Josh were going to meet them. As Sarah peeped around Jake's shoulder, she saw her friends, Cassie and Josh waiting by the oak tree. She waved, and Cassie waved back.

Cassie and Josh stood to greet their friends as they all rolled off the hill parking in front of them. Jake quickly said a "hey" for everyone. It was evident that something was on his mind. He didn't want to take the time for casual talk. He needed to talk about what had just occurred on Gamble Farm. "Did you guys see anything strange on your side of Gamble Farm?" he asked Will, Lindsey, Josh, and Cassie.

They were as eager to talk about it as Jake. Will declared, "I couldn't believe my eyes! What is going on at Gamble Farm that would warrant guards to surround the property? That was what we saw, wasn't it?"

Most of the friends nodded in agreement. "That's the only thing I can think it could be?" Seth mused, "What do you think, Jake?"

Jake nodded, "I don't know what else it could

have been."

Sarah spoke, "One of the men spotted us. I saw him looking straight at Jake and me as we were leaving. I waved at him, and he waved back."

They all turned toward her with their mouths open expectantly. She looked from one to the other and finally spoke, "Well, I didn't know what else to do so I acted like the most common thing on Buffalo Creek is to see an army of dark-clad men guarding a farm that has been vacant forever."

Everyone stared at her, and she stared back, "What?" she demanded. Jake was the first to burst out laughing with the rest following suit. Sarah joined in, and when everyone finished laughing, their eyes were wet with tears. Cassie and Josh joined in the laughter although they had no idea why they were laughing.

Cassie wiped her face free of tears and asked, "What did you do that got everyone on your case, Sarah?"

Sarah realized that Cassie and Josh had missed their unwelcoming at Gamble Farm. She began telling the two what they had observed while coming over the ridge. Cassie and Josh listened with intent interest and a glimpse of sadness as they realized their hang out spot had been taken from them.

Josh asked, "So the new guy moved onto the farm? I met him yesterday. He was polite enough. I asked him if he would like to hang out with us sometime, and he said maybe once he was settled. I got the feeling he isn't much of a team kind of guy. I'll bet he's a loner. But he seemed nice enough."

Jake, was curious, "Did you find out anything about him? Like why his family moved to the head of Buffalo Creek?"

"No, he didn't say a word about himself. He didn't ask me about our town or us or anything, either. He acted as if he wasn't interested in any of what Salyersville has to offer."

"Or, maybe, he knows all he needs to know," mumbled Will. He had a look of unease as he stood listening to the conversation. Sarah looked around the group and saw the same look on each of her friends' faces.

"Guys, it isn't our business. Just because we

have new neighbors that are different from the other locals doesn't mean they are dangerous. We are overreacting because we're losing our playground. Let's just vow to make the new neighbors welcome to their new community." She looked from one to the other, and slowly they all agreed to make a special effort to make the new guy feel welcomed.

"Enough of this talkin'." Jake exclaimed. "Let's forget this stuff and ride." He revved his engine and motioned for Sarah to join him. Everyone took his lead and mounted their four-wheelers and off they went. It didn't take long for them to forget the suspicious incident of the morning. The excitement of the climb and the wind on their faces helped to make the day carefree. Sarah was so blissfully content.

Around 12 o'clock they stopped on top of the highest hill they had climbed and spread out their blankets for lunch. They kidded each other and played around as usual. Cassie and Josh sat close to each other, no doubt dreading the summer separation as much as Sarah and Jake were. Sarah tried not to cling to Jake, but couldn't help herself. Jake didn't seem to mind that she was stuck so close to him all day.

Sarah noticed that Isabelle and Seth were staying close also. Maybe those two would make a good, solid couple by the end of the summer. She was sure they were headed in that direction. Sarah was happy they were all comfortable with each other. She looked from one couple to the other, and just for a brief moment thought about how much she would miss their rides during the summer.

She shook her mood away and turned to Josh. "How are you spending your time while Cassie is with her dad, Josh?" She knew Josh would miss Cassie. It was obvious to her and the rest of their friends that Cassie and Josh were totally into each other.

Josh looked over at Cassie and then his good friend, Sarah. "Well, I guess I'll just hang around here and work on the farms to earn some extra cash. What about you?"

"I'm going to work at my mom's clinic with the animals. I can use the experience and the cash she'll pay me." She laughed. Her mom was a stickler about paying Sarah just as she would for any summer worker who worked for her. "I guess we are the only ones left in Salyersville for the summer." She looked at the others. Everyone was going to be gone for part of the summer, either at the beginning, or at the end.

"Jake, are you excited about your summer at UK? I can't believe you snagged a spot in that program. Don't you get a chance to go again next year?" Josh asked.

Jake's face lit up. "Yep. I get to go this summer and then again next summer, and if I decide UK is the school for me, I'll have an opportunity to go to summer school free during my freshman year. I'm totally pumped."

Seth picked up on the conversation, "Wow, a doctor in the family; I'm proud, bro!" He noticed Jake's sheepish smile, and he interrupted what he thought was Jake's comeback. "No, I'm serious. I am proud, man."

Jake, uncomfortable with the attention everyone was paying him, turned the focus toward Seth. "So, Seth, what are you up to this summer?"

"I'm going to Washington D.C. to spend the summer with my brother. I thought since he's so close to the Capitol and Virginia Beach; I might as well take advantage."

"What about you, Cameron? What's your plan for the summer?" Jake pulled their other friend into the conversation. "And, what are you up to this summer, Isabelle?"

Isabelle was visibly pleased to be included in the conversation. She hesitated for a moment and when Cameron didn't offer up his plan she began telling what she would be doing. "I'm going to work at the pharmacy in Highland's Regional for the summer. I think that I want to study Pharmacy, and I'm hoping that working in the hospital pharmacy will help me make up my mind."

"Cam, that leaves you. What's up for the summer?" pressed Jake.

Cameron shrugged his shoulders. "I'm not sure yet. I think I'll be working on the farms same as Josh; making some money for college next year."

Cassie piped up, "I'll only be away for four weeks and then back home with my mom and my friends. I'll so miss you guys. I can't believe that only last year my whole goal was to find a way to get Mom to move back to Louisville. Now, I only want it to go as quickly as possible so that I can get back to my life here. Things have a way of changing on you." She marveled.

Sarah agreed. But, she didn't want things to change. She loved her life just the way it was. Alas, she had to grow up and take what came her way. Being away from her boyfriend for eight weeks was not the end of the world. She had to keep telling herself that.

Will said he was going to hang around and just see what happened or in other words; he was going to hang out at the pool again this year as a lifeguard. They all knew he would end up there, he always did. He loved it, but the boys gave him so much grief because of the little tweens that always got a crush on him.

Will was ready to change the conversation. "Let's ride, boys!"

"Hey!" Cassie protested.

"Sorry. Boys and girls let's ride," he revised.

They gathered the blankets and cleaned up their picnic spot. It was easy since the food was gone. With their crew, there were no leftovers, not even for the animals. They made a second scan making sure they didn't leave something that would hurt the cattle or horses. After they had finished cleaning up, they were off to enjoy riding the rest of the afternoon.

When the evening crept upon them, they said goodbye to Cassie and Josh as they headed off the hill to the Howard's Farm. The rest of the group started toward the ridge that led them to Gamble's Farm. When Jake remembered the morning incident, he slowed down to ask the others what they wanted to do. "Should we hit the hill above and take the long way home since we felt nervous about passing by Gamble Farm this morning?"

"I vote to take the long way," Sarah stated. "They obviously don't want company so why push it?"

"She's right," Seth agreed.

Cameron turned his four-wheeler toward the hill beside the ridge they were on as an answer. They would forgo their regular route today. They rode in silence. Their carefree mood slowly drained from the beautiful, wonderful day.

The hill was rougher than usual and the view was not as beautiful as their favorite trail, but it was still nice with the mature trees and greenery. Sarah loved the woods. She was content on the back of a four-wheeler or the back of a horse. She might live in the backwoods of Eastern Kentucky, but she loved her community and the people in her neighborhood--at least, until now.

Would Samuel and his family cause a change in her little town? She prayed that things on Buffalo Creek stayed the same. She had an eerie feeling that her home and life were about to change, and not for the good.

Sarah and Jake bid their friends goodbye as they started down the hill toward the barn. They were just in time to feed the livestock and do Sarah's chores. Then they made their way to Jake's barn and did his chores. They mounted the four-wheeler one last time, and Jake dropped Sarah off so she could get ready for their date to the movies. She had wanted to see the latest James Bond movie for weeks and finally they were going.

Actually, if she were honest, she'd have to admit that she really didn't care if the movie was good or not, she wanted one last date with Jake. The movie was a good excuse to have a night out with him.

FIVE

While sitting in Showtime Movie Theater, Sarah's thoughts once again slipped into the same gloomy place they had resided in lately. This movie would be the last movie they would see together until school started next year. Dang, why did she keep allowing herself to get to this depth of gloom? She had to make herself stop. Jake was still there sitting beside her, and she wanted to enjoy every second she had with him. She reached over and took his hand in hers. Jake gently placed a kiss on their two entwined hands. Life was good tonight; she would think of summer later.

After the movies, Jake dropped her off at home promising to see her the next day at church. She gave him a kiss and ran into her house. Once she was inside, she leaned against the door and allowed fatigue to wash over her. Maybe, if she was this tired, she would sleep without her brain dancing until the wee hours of the night thinking about Jake's leaving.

She slipped into her bed and resolved to think of seeing Jake at church tomorrow. She settled into bed, but instead of thinking of Jake, she found herself thinking of Samuel and his family.

Why was this stranger taking up precious time she could be thinking of Jake? Why did he keep creeping into her thoughts? It must be because he was a stranger in town. Not only was he a stranger, but he was just a bit strange. Why would anyone have men that looked like the mafia guarding their farm? A farm in the foothills of Eastern Kentucky didn't warrant the need of protection. What does someone protect on a rundown farm on Buffalo Creek? Sarah shook her head. The new neighbor on Buffalo Creek was definitely on the strange side. She forced Jake back into her thoughts and went to sleep thinking of how much she loved her boyfriend.

The next day Sarah found Jake saving her a seat in the same spot they had occupied for as long as they had attended Licking River Baptist Church. While they sat listening to the message, Sarah noticed Samuel sitting two pews in front of them. How odd, Samuel was sitting by himself. Where was his family?

Sarah searched the church for strangers but found no one that she didn't already know. Samuel must have come to church by himself.

After church, Jake took Sarah to Joe's Pizza Place, next door to the bowling alley. Seth and Isabelle were there and asked Sarah and Jake to join them. It felt good sitting with the new couple. Seth was smiling from ear to ear and Isabelle couldn't keep her eyes off him.

While eating their pizza, Jake nudged Sarah. She followed his eyes. Standing at the counter was Samuel. He was ordering a pizza to go. Was he going to eat all by himself? Sarah leaned into Jake. "Should we invite him to join us? I mean, he is our neighbor."

Jake took his cue. "Samuel." Samuel turned around searching for the origin of the call. He spotted the two couples sitting in the corner and half-heartedly waved.

Seth offered, "Hey, neighbor, want to join us? We have plenty of room."

Samuel hesitated. Finally, he nodded and strolled over to their table. "Hello." He shook hands with Jake and Seth while nodding to Isabelle and Sarah. "I met Sarah the other day, but I don't think I've met the rest of you. Did you say we are neighbors?"

Seth nodded. "Yep, you have entered the Creekers Club. If you live on the Creek, you're one of us. We all live around Lick Creek and Buffalo Creek hence the Creeker Club." He was proud of himself for thinking of the name on the cuff and he searched his friends' faces for their approval. When no one said anything he offered, "Get it, Creekers Club?" When no one said anything, his face dropped in disappointment. But not for long. Everyone started laughing. Seth joined in the laughter at his own expense, "You guys."

Samuel watched the friends as they laughed and seemed so comfortable with each other. He nodded. "Glad to meet everyone." He smiled with a polite smile that seemed well practiced.

Sarah noticed the stiffness in his conversation once again. He was polite enough but didn't allow his guard down. She didn't miss his reference to their earlier meeting. The boys took over the conversation. They began telling Samuel the ends and outs of Lick Creek and Buffalo Creek. They told him about the group of friends that lived on Lick Creek and Buffalo Creek.

Jake offered, "As a matter of fact, we take long rides on our horses or our four-wheelers in the woods near your farm on the weekends. If you're interested, you should join us on our next ride."

Samuel politely agreed that he would indeed join them on the ride next time they went. "Just alert me before and I'll be ready. Thank you for inviting me."

The remainder of the gathering was polite, yet the fun had dwindled. Positive that it was the newness of their new neighbor, Sarah refused to think that Samuel wouldn't fit into their little group. Although they were a tight knit group, they welcomed anyone into their circle. He just had to get acquainted with them and their silliness.

After watching Isabelle's attentiveness with Seth, Sarah determined that she liked Isabelle, and she approved of her friend dating this girl. Later, she told Jake as much while he'd chuckled. "I'm sure Seth will be relieved that you give your seal of approval."

She laughed. "Well, I liked Cassie from the beginning and look how well that has turned out for Josh." She looked at Jake, "Do you regret, that we never had that moment where we met and had to discover if we liked each other or not?"

Jake took a long look at her, "I wouldn't trade one thing from the moment we met while in our diapers till this very moment with you. God has been good to us, Sarah. His gift to us is allowing us to find each other early in life."

Sarah's eyes filled with tears. She couldn't think of a reply. She beamed at Jake. He ever so gently picked up her hand and kissed the back of it. He laid it back in her lap and caressed her face and lightly kissed the tip of her nose. "I love you, Sarah."

"I love you back, Jake." She wrapped her arms around him and held on for the longest time. Life stood still for the moment, and they just were. "I love you and don't you forget it while you're studying all the parts of the human body." she finally managed to say.

On their way home Jake asked, "What did you think about Samuel today?" He glanced over to see if

Sarah was listening.

She nodded. "Wonder what he thought about us?" She wrinkled her brow, "He is very uptight. Don't you think?" She looked at Jake, "Don't you think it's funny that he was attending church by himself? Where were his parents?"

Jake nodded, "He isn't the happiest person I know. But we'll take care of that. Now that he's a Creeker." He looked at Sarah desperately trying to not burst into laughter from his use of Seth's new term for them. Finally, they both allowed their laugh to fill the truck. Then they were back into their own thoughts. The two sat in silence the rest of the way home. Neither of them knew what to make of their new neighbor.

They sat in Jake's Chevy in front of her house for a long time even though they had school tomorrow. It was the last week of school and finals were upon them. She had to go in, and they both had to rest for their testing tomorrow. "Rest well and I'll see you after my Biology final," she whispered.

Jake cringed, "you know how to bring a guy

back to earth, don't you? The last thing I want to think about while I have my girl in my arms is my finals!" He pushed her out the door of the truck and jumped out on his side. They walked arm in arm up the sidewalk. "See you tomorrow. Ace your test and I'll ace mine. Deal?"

"Deal," she breathed as she drew his mouth to her own. After a long minute, she made her lips pull from Jake and watched as he turned, ran down the sidewalk, and leaped into his truck. He waved and was gone. Sarah opened the heavy wooden door and floated to her bedroom, thanking God for her wonderful life..

SIX

Finals week sped by too fast for Sarah. She knew that everyone was ready for the school year to be over, but she wanted to scream for time to slow down. It was going by way too fast. She wanted to absorb every moment of the time she had left with Jake.

Unfortunately, their last week of school was coming to an end. The positive on the ending of the school year was that the weekend was near. Josh and Cassie invited Sarah and Jake to go horseback riding on the Johnson Farm in celebration of the end of the school year. Sarah loved riding on the Johnson Farm. The land was perfect for riding. The trails that hugged the hills and valleys on the farm made riding in the woods interesting, but not dangerous. The best part was visiting with Mammy, Josh's great-grandmother. Josh's family had owned the farm for many generations, and his great-grandmother still lived in a small house not far from Josh's family's residence.

The friends loved Mammy and enjoyed visiting

with her. She was an ancient lady with a grand sense of humor who loved having company. She always told them stories about the past and secrets that only she knew about their families. The best part was that she always had a dessert baked for them. Mammy was in her happiest mood when the teens came for a visit. She loved her great-grandson and his friends. Her joy was obvious from the light in her eyes when they sat down at her table and inhaled her desserts.

Sarah remembered how Mammy helped Cassie and Josh when it looked like Cassie was going to move back to Louisville. Even though her friend Cassie had lived in Louisville until last year, her mother had grown up in Salyersville, and her roots were on the farm she lived on now. Cassie's great-grandparents left their farm to their granddaughter, Cassie's mom. The mother and daughter had promptly left Louisville to make Salyersville their home.

When the Wards moved into their home, they soon realized that something or someone was occupying the house with them. When Cassie's mom realized that there was something paranormal about their home she was ready to move Cassie back to

Louisville. That's when Josh and Cassie had turned to Mammy for help in understanding what was happening in the home. Mammy revealed stories about the house that Cassie's great-grandparents had told her.

After talking about the house with Mammy, they realized what or who was occupying the house with Cassie and her mother. Mammy told them about the lady that once lived in the house and the rumors of her demise by her husband.

It was a hard time for Cassie and Josh. Their relationship was in danger because of the threat of the lingering soul occupying the house. But, thanks to Josh's parents and to Mark Caudill, a friend of Cassie's mom, they determined that the house was safe. So, when all was said and done, Cassie and her mother decided to stay on the farm and share the house with the lady ghost. It'd been a year, and although strange incidents still occurred on occasion, overall the house had settled and Cassie and her mom were happy.

Today, the four friends planned to ride over to Josh's for a visit with Mammy. Sarah was excited because it would give her a chance to ride Heine on the trail for the first time. He was ready, and Sarah was anxious to see him work the trail. "Are you riding over to the house and then we'll leave from the barn?"

"I think so. Can you get Heine ready on your own?" Jake's face held a mock concerned frown.

She pretended to weigh whether she could handle getting her horse ready to ride or whether she would need a big strong man to help. She giggled. "Of course I can handle my horse! If I can't get him ready, who will help me when you leave me for the whole summer?"

Her words just slipped out, and she wished she could pull them back into her mouth. She watched Jake's face cloud over and she felt guilty for making him feel bad. "I'm sorry. My big mouth. Let's just enjoy this wonderful afternoon with good friends and fine horses, okay?"

Jake's mood lightened. "That sounds like a country music song." He began singing in a twangy country voice, "*Good friends and fine horses…*" They both laughed. He couldn't think of what line should come next. "I think I need Brad Paisley's help on this one.

Sarah allowed her mood to lighten, too. She was excited to ride her horse and spend a carefree day with her friends. She looked forward to hearing tales of Lick Creek and Buffalo Creek that Mammy was sure to tell them. Mammy made their little community sound exciting and full of mystery. The Lick Creek and Buffalo Creek that Mammy told stories about was certainly different from the place where Sarah had lived in her whole life. To her, Salyersville was the same boring place with nothing exciting ever happening.

She couldn't think of anything interesting that had happened while she'd lived on Buffalo Creek. She winkled her nose. At least nothing that would rank as exciting except for Cassie's house with it's lady ghost. She wondered when her little neighborhood had become so boring since it had been full of excitement back in Mammy's time.

SEVEN

Sarah was ready and waiting for Jake when he arrived riding his beautiful horse, George. She swung her body on top of Heine and they were ready to ride. They trotted off toward the ridge they had climbed on their four-wheeler just days before.

Once on top of the ridge, Jake slowed George. "Let's take a new route. We don't want to disturb the hoodlums again." Sarah nodded as she nudged Heine to change directions.

They turned the horses toward an adjoining hill and found a path the cattle had left. They climbed the hill and rode around to the other side and back down again. Cassie and Josh were waiting at their usual meeting place, ready to run their horses over to the Johnson Farm. Heine was doing well. Sarah was happy with her new horse. He stood tall and majestic.

Just looking at him was breathtaking. He was dark and mysterious. The only marking he had was a ring around both of his front hooves and a white spot on his nose. Cassie and Josh both remarked on how beautiful Heine looked while coming down the trail.

Jake, not one to take the back seat, interrupted, "Hey, what about old George here? He didn't look bad coming down that trail." He rubbed George's neck and side as he spoke. They all laughed. George was a good looking animal, and he could rank with Heine, but Jake's need to voice it at that moment, as if George was getting his feelings hurt from listening to the praise for Heine was hilarious.

Josh turned serious, "Let's go back up to the ridge and go east toward the Gamble Farm. We can hit the ridge from that point. It'll save wear and tear on the horses going up and down all the hills."

Sarah felt uneasy. "Are we sure we want to get that close to the Gamble place since it has new owners, and not so friendly ones at that?"

Josh shook his head, "What are they going to do? We won't trespass on their land. We're only going next to their property line to save our horses some steps." He looked at Sarah and then at Jake.

Jake finally relented, "You're right. What are they going to do? We can't allow them to scare us from our territory, right? Are we going to stay away from the trail forever?" He turned his horse and moved toward the hill to begin, retracing his steps. Sarah followed, but she still had a weird feeling in the pit of her stomach. Cassie followed Sarah, and Josh brought up the back.

Once the horses carried them close to the Gamble property line, Sarah felt her heart begin pounding. She scolded herself for being silly. She tried to push her apprehension away and enjoy the surrounding woods. They rode around the property line for ten minutes and nothing. The dark clad men were nowhere to be seen. Maybe they had been determining what needed to be done to the farm to make it productive again. For some reason, Sarah doubted that the men in dark suits had any idea of what to do on a farm. She tried to stop thinking and just ride. She found herself stealing glances toward the farm. Nothing was different with the trees and land they had played on just weeks ago.

Yet, everything had changed. They were not welcome on the land anymore nor would they ever be welcomed.

Something interrupted her thoughts. She heard the sound of galloping hoof beats coming toward them. She breathed, "Run!" Her friends, thinking she had seen something, picked up the pace of their horses to a gallop. The faster they moved the faster the sounds moved toward them. Just when they thought they'd lost their pursuer and they slowed down, they heard a voice shout sharply, "Sarah."

Sarah's jump on Heine's back making him nervous. She anxiously looked back toward the sound. She was prepared to see one of the dark-clad men; maybe the one that she had waved at before. Instead, she saw Samuel riding the most beautiful white horse. He pulled his horse close to the four and greeted them with a nod of his head. The boys did the same, and Sarah said, "Hi, Samuel. I didn't realize you were following us." She surprised herself with how calm her voice sounded.

Samuel looked at them and replied, "I wasn't following you. I live here, remember?"

"Of course, I guess I wasn't thinking." Sarah stammered. Jake made his way back to Sarah's side. Samuel didn't miss the subtlety of his move.

"I called for you since your name is the only one I remembered." He smiled at the rest of the group. "So you guys are out for a ride this morning?"

Sarah took charge, "We're headed to Josh's Mammy's for a visit." She noticed Samuel's quizzical look at Cassie and Josh. "I'm sorry. You probably haven't met Cassie and Josh yet." She motioned to Cassie, "My best friend, Cassie Ward. She lives on the farm just west of your farm." Cassie nodded toward Samuel with a welcoming smile, and he nodded back. Josh moved his horse close to Cassie and Sarah got the hint, "Her boyfriend, Josh Johnson. He lives on the Johnson Farm on the other side of Cassie's farm." Sarah smiled at Jake. " You know my boyfriend, Jake. He lives down at the mouth of the creek on the Gullett Farm."

Both boys nodded toward Samuel. Jake offered, "How're you doing today, Samuel? That is some horse you have there. He's a beauty."

Samuel gave Jake a cold smile, "Thank you, Jake."

Josh joined in the discussion, "Samuel, we met the other day in the hallway outside of Mrs. Patrick's room. We talked for a while…"

Samuel's facial expression didn't change, but his eyes moved to Josh. "Yes, I remember you, Josh. I just didn't get your name the other day."

Cassie offered, "Well, now you've met the gang, Samuel. Welcome to Buffalo Creek. We'd love to make you feel at home. Would you like to join us on our ride?"

Jake offered, "We'd love to have you ride with us."

Josh added, "We're headed to my Mammy's to have some of her delicious cookin'. You don't want to miss any of her food. Eating Mammy's food will be a grand welcome to the Creek for you."

Samuel looked at Sarah and then at the rest of the group. "I must give my apologies. I do wish I could join you, but I need to be back on the farm by 12 o'clock, and so I must say good-bye. Nice meeting everyone." And with that, he turned his horse and rode toward the barn that looked like it had seen much better days.

The couples watched as Samuel's long straight form on his white horse slowly rode away. As Sarah watched, her curiosity heightened. Who was this secretive person that kept popping into their lives?

Josh voiced Sarah's thoughts. "Who is this guy that keeps showing up when we least expect him?"

Sarah surprised herself by calling after Samuel. "Samuel, why don't you go with us? We promise to have you back here by 12 o'clock. That way you can get a small glimpse of what the Creek has to offer a horse rider like you."

Josh backed Sarah's invite with an invitation. "Come on, Samuel. You don't want to miss my Mammy's sweet pies and cakes."

Samuel relented, "Okay, I'll tell my staff that I'll be out for a while and meet up with you on the trail in a few minutes."

Jake nodded, "We'll go slow so you can catch

up."

Samuel nodded and turned back toward the barn and was gone. The four looked on with a puzzled look. Cassie broke the trance they were in and moved slowly on the trail with Josh following her. Sarah and Jake followed the other couple without talking. They seemed to be taking in the new neighbor's rigid façade. Friendly but distant.

Josh pulled to a stop, and everyone followed suit. "We should probably wait for him. This opening should be far enough away for his privacy. I think he wanted to get us away from the farm. Did anyone else get that feeling?"

Jake mused, "He is certainly different. He acts like he is protecting the property from us. I can't put my finger on it, but it is strange."

"This is his property," Cassie reminded. "Like it or not, his family owns this land to do as they please."

Jake changed the subject with a moan. "I hope he gets here soon. I can almost hear Mammy's apple pie calling my name." He cocked his head sideways allowing his ear to listen to the wind.

Just as everyone laughed, Samuel appeared. "Thank you for inviting me. I haven't gotten to explore the area yet." He pulled his horse close to Jake's and slowed.

"Good to have you, friend." Jake offered, trying to cut through Samuel's businesslike manner.

Cassie pulled her horse in front of the others and began the ride to the corner hollow. "Come on, let's get to Johnson Farm and visit Mammy." The rest of the group followed her. They soon forgot their new neighbor and his family invasion of the Gamble Farm. They were at ease with their horses and the woods surrounding them.

Sarah stole several glances of Samuel as they rode, trying to decide what made him tick. He was formal and evasive all the time. She didn't want to be snobbish toward their neighbor. After all, his family was part of them now. Each time she chanced a look, Samuel was a blank canvas. He didn't seem unhappy or disturbed in any way, but he didn't show any joy or humor either. Their new neighbor was definitely a strange stranger.

Once they had ridden down to the hollow between the Howard and Johnson farms, they began picking up the pace. Jake, now in front of everyone, shouted, "Let's race!" Josh had anticipated his friend's challenge and had already picked up the pace on his horse. Samuel nudged his white horse to a gallop and off they went. The girls allowed the boys to run ahead while they moved slower, laughing as the boys disappeared into the trees.

"I'm going to miss this so much!" Sarah moaned.

Cassie stopped her horse and leaned over to her friend. "It's for a short time, Sarah. Jake will be happier if you support him during this time. Allow him to develop his skills without worrying about you back here." She nudged her horse to quicken their pace. "I won't be gone long, only three maybe four weeks. I'll be home, and we'll make the summer fun. Okay?"

Sarah looked at her friend and nodded, pushing her bad mood away. "You are the best friend, Cassie. I am so glad you're here. Yes, we will make this a good summer. I'm going to make sure Jake knows this so he won't worry about my summer while he's studying in

Lexington." She nudged Heine, and they began a quick pace to catch up with the boys.

When they came in sight of Mammy's house, they saw the boys' horses resting outside in the front yard. They left their horses with the guys' horses and walked up the steps to the front door. The door was open, and as they came to the screened door, Sarah called "Mammy. Do you want more company?"

The house was uncharacteristically silent. Usually, you could hear Mammy's laughter in the yard. Sarah knocked on the open door and walked inside the house. When they entered, they saw Mammy sitting in her chair looking like she had seen a ghost. Samuel and Jake were standing near, not knowing what to do next. Cassie ran over to her, "Mammy, are you okay? What can we get you?"

Josh came running from the kitchen with a large glass of water. "Here Mammy, drink this. You must have been working too hard this morning." His face was drawn with concern for the old woman he loved. He took one of the catalogs from her side table and began fanning her.

Mammy, realizing that her great-grandson and his friends were worried about her, collected her composure. "Josh, you quit acting like I'm an old woman. I'm okay. I just saw this young man and he made me go back to my youth." She took a drink of the water Josh had given her, and her beady eyes pierced Samuel's face. Samuel, for once, was showing emotions. He was obviously uncomfortable with Mammy's reaction to him. The others were also feeling uncomfortable with Mammy's response.

Josh tried to bring the moment back to normal. "Mammy, you seem to know Samuel." He looked at Mammy and then at Samuel. "Samuel, do you know my Mammy from somewhere?"

Samuel shook his head no. He didn't say a word. Just stared at Mammy's face. He backed away from the front of the group to stand behind Sarah and Cassie. Almost as if he was ready to flee at a moments notice.

Josh tried again, "Mammy, this is our new neighbor, Samuel. His family bought the Gamble farm."

They heard the old woman's attempt at a giggle and then, "Oh my, I am sorry, son. You look so much like an old beau of mine from years ago. Strange, you could be his twin. Except he's about eighty years older than you and he's been gone for a very long time now." She looked down at her wrinkled hands, "Your likeness to him startled me. Where are you from, Samuel? Maybe you're kin to him."

Samuel visually relaxed. "I'm from Connecticut, Ma'am. I'm afraid I don't know anyone from around here. I only met these guys recently."

Mammy recovered quickly, "Well, glad to have you. Come in here and find a seat. I've got lots to eat. You better hurry, these boys will eat up all the apple pie if you aren't quick." Her dry, cracked laugh put them all at ease and Josh and Jake began pushing each other away from the table trying to get the first piece of pie.

Mammy shooed them away. "Mind your manners now boys. The first slice goes to Samuel here. Sit down right here Samuel and I'll cut you a good size piece. You do like apple pie don't you?"

Samuel smiled the first genuine smile Sarah had seen from him. "Yes, I love apple pie. And I heard you make the best."

Mammy laughed, "Yep, that's what they tell me. And if these boys are any indication it must be true. Although I'm pretty sure they would eat it no matter what it tastes like." She laughed her joyous laugh once again. She motioned Josh and Jake to sit and served them their pieces too.

Sarah and Cassie made their way to Mammy's table to find Josh and Jake already eating huge pieces of apple pie with large glasses of milk. Samuel was politely waiting for the girls to sit.

Josh noticed Samuel waiting and slowed shoveling the pie into his mouth. "Samuel, if you wait for those girls you won't get to eat all you want of Mammy's cookin'. They will only eat one piece." He patted his belly. "You know they watch their figures." He batted his eyes and laughed. He looked at Sarah and Cassie and tried to correct himself. "And might I add, they do have the best figures you'll ever find."

Jake swallowed his pie and laughed. "Nice save

buddy boy." He winked at Sarah. "But he has a point, Samuel. Waiting for these two will cost you some serious pie eating time." And he demonstrated by shoveling a large spoonful into his mouth.

Mammy patted Samuel on his back. "Don't pay any attention to these two. They're always trying to make me feel good about my cookin' so that I'll keep feedin' 'em." Mammy was already cutting two more pieces of pie for the girls, and they had no intention of saying no to Mammy's delicious pie.

Samuel took a huge bite of pie and quickly exclaimed, "This is delicious, Mammy. I knew it would be good. These guys promised me that it would be delicious, but I wasn't prepared for how good this taste." Mammy's beady eyes still searching Samuel's features, patted his back. "Thank you, young man."

Sarah knew that Josh had told Mammy they might stop by, and she had made the pies just for their visit. She and Cassie both praised the pie as they dug into the hot syrup filled crust. Mammy's wrinkled face was radiant with the pleasure of serving her young company. Her great-grandson and his friends mirrored her pleasure. They loved visiting Mammy, eating her delicious cooking and listening to her stories of the past.

Once the five were settled and shoveling pie into their faces, Mammy shuffled her old legs over to an empty chair at the dining table. She slowly sat down and faced her young company. She watched as they gobbled down the last of their pie. All the while, asking if anyone would have seconds. Josh, Jake, and Samuel had seconds at least three times. It was a good thing Mammy had made several pies.

Josh looked at Samuel as they began their third piece of pie, "Didn't I tell you? My Mammy can cook." He finished with a large bite of pie.

Samuel took a bite of his pie and nodded. "That you did, and you are right. This is without a doubt the best pie I've ever eaten." He smiled at Mammy.

Mammy was trying to stop staring at Samuel, but they all couldn't keep from noticing her obvious staring. Samuel was dealing with it all well. It was almost as if he enjoyed the attention of the old woman. He smiled at Mammy and gave her all of his attention during the visit.

Between bites, Josh asked, "Mammy, is there anything you can tell Samuel about Gamble Farm? Are there any stories that'd interest the new owners?"

Mammy smiled and got a faraway look on her face. She seemed to be somewhere else for a moment. They assumed she was thinking of stories she could tell about Gamble Farm. She loved a good story. But instead of telling them some history that only she could tell, she replied, "No, I can't remember much about the old farm. Just that it's run down settin' up there on that hill without anyone livin' there. Maybe your family will breathe new life into it, Samuel." She looked Samuel up and down before finishing. "It's amazin' how much you look like Sam. He lived on your farm many years ago. A young man, and if I might say so, one good lookin' man." Once again Mammy's memories took her away while visiting the past.

Josh gulped a swig of milk, "Who was this Sam, Mammy? It sounds like you might have cared more than just him being your beau. What happened between the two of you?"

Mammy's beady eyes pierced Josh's face.

"What?" Josh's words brought her back to the young people at her table. "Me and Sam didn't have a chance. He was killed not long after we were tryin' to court each other." She hesitated, "Samuel, have you heard any stories about your house? You know how people make up tales."

Samuel shook his head no since his mouth was full of pie. He was curious about his new farm. "What kind of tales, Mammy?"

Mammy just shook her head. She wasn't ready to tell them any more than she had already said. Sarah was sure that Mammy had stories she could tell them about the farm, but didn't push the old woman to give up what she knew. If Mammy wanted to tell them, she would do it without being pushed to do so.

Mammy studied Samuel's face, the wisdom of her years showing on her face as she weighed what she should say. "Who found this farm for you to buy, Samuel?"

Samuel gulped his milk and answered, "Well, my father bought it while I was away at school. So, I don't know how he found it."

Mammy pierced Samuel's face with her beady eyes. "What did you say your last name is Samuel?"

Samuel offered, "Lazra."

Mammy looked off into the distance trying to remember something. "Lazra. That name rings a bell. I can't put my finger on it, but I've heard that name somewhere." She snorted, "It's one that a body wouldn't forget once they've heard it." She looked off into the kitchen as if commanding her brain to retrieve the information. After a few moments, she shook her head and sighed. "I just can't figure out where I've heard that name before."

Mammy, still curious, asked, "And what's your parents' names?"

Samuel answered, "My mother's name is Belinda and my father is Palmer."

Mammy whispered to herself, "Belinda and Palmer Lazra." She finally gave up, shaking her head free of the names she brought her attention back to the young people sitting at her dining table.

Once Jake, Josh, and Samuel had finished off

three whole pies, the group said their goodbyes to Mammy, mounted up and rode off toward home. Samuel stopped on top of the ridge and as if guarding them, waited until the couples were out of eyesight from his farm before making his way to the barn. Once alone, Samuel smiled allowing Mammy's reaction to him and her questions to marinate while he took care of his horse.

The group split at Samuel's ridge while Josh went with Cassie to her barn to put her horse up and Jake and Sarah headed for Sarah's farm to take care of their horses. Sarah was quiet on the trail home. Once they got close to the barn, Jake offered, "Penny for your thoughts."

"I was just thinking of Mammy's reaction to Samuel. I've never seen her react to someone like that. Didn't you think it was odd?"

Jake nodded, "I know. She was infatuated with Samuel. And I think Samuel liked her, too. He warmed up to her a lot more than he does with us."

Sarah agreed. "Yeah, he didn't seem to mind her staring at him at all."

They finished in the barn, and Jake mounted his horse, promising to be back at Sarah's early the next morning since they only had tomorrow and then the day of his departure would be upon them. They hadn't made any plans for Saturday. They just wanted to hang out together for the day.

That's just what they did. They sat outside at the pool for a long time and then made their way to the barns. Jake stayed late, and no one argued that he was not allowed to be at Sarah's that late at night.

When he finally pulled away from Sarah and kissed her goodbye, the tears that had been threatening to spill all day fell and mixed. Sarah felt as if a hole inside her heart had emptied, leaving her soul to swivel up and die. She made her way up to her bedroom trying to be quiet, not wanting her parents to know how broken her heart felt. She got ready for bed with tears streaming down her face. She found her pillow and buried her head to muffle her sobs. Her best friend-- Her other half was leaving, and she was alone. For the first time in her life, she was alone without Jake.

Sunday came, and Jake packed his truck and said his goodbyes to his parents. His family was okay with his absence for the summer. They knew how much this meant to him. One last time, his mother spouted out her list of things for him to do while gone. He'd heard them over and over for the past week, but he listened and assured her that he would keep his toothbrush in its container so germs wouldn't get on it from the community bathroom he would be using. He agreed to wear flip-flops in the community shower, and he would change his bed sheets once a week. He promised and nodded for at least five minutes while packing the last of his things in the truck. He kissed his mom and his dad goodbye and headed up the road to Sarah's.

Now was the moment he had been dreading. He stopped in Sarah's driveway. He waited by his truck while the girl he loved walked toward him. As he watched her slowly move toward him, he couldn't help but admire her beauty. He was a lucky man. He had the love of a beautiful woman. They would make it through this, and they would be stronger for it.

Sarah was determined to keep strong. It wasn't as if Jake would be gone forever. She met him while he lounged by the door of his truck with a smile on his face. She admiringly took a picture in her mind of his handsome body leaned against his truck. She knew in her heart that they would be okay. She knew that Jake cared for her as much as she cared for him. She leaned into him and kissed him. He pulled his arms around her and pulled her close. She felt the urgency of his hold. She melted into him and held on for dear life.

Finally, she pulled away from him, surprised that she was the strong one at this moment. She smiled at him, "I'm going to count this as the first day of my countdown until you are home. I can mark it on my calendar tonight."

Jake pulled her hand to his chest and allowed his breath to release. He then reminded Sarah, "Remember, at 4 o'clock every afternoon no matter what we are doing we'll stop and think of each other for at least fifteen minutes. Agreed?"

Sarah pulled her arms around his neck and looked into his eyes, "Agreed."

They kissed a slow, gentle kiss and then he was gone--gone for eight whole weeks. Sarah felt lonelier than she had ever felt in her entire life. She found her way to her room through her tears and slumped onto her bed, wishing she could go back to sleep to stop the hurt for a moment.

EIGHT

Just as she began to fade into sleep, her phone rang. It was Cassie. Of course, her best friend would be there to help her through this horrible time. "Hi, Cassie," Sarah clung to the phone, "he's gone." Her voice quivered even though she tried hard to keep her voice even. "I miss him already."

Cassie invited Sarah over to have a movie night with her mom and her. Sarah wasn't sure if she should go given the mood she was in, but Cassie pleaded. She decided she might as well get used to being without Jake, so she forced herself to get up off her bed. She wiped her eyes and made her legs move. She made her way downstairs to the kitchen where she found her mother. "Mom, Cassie asked me to come over for movie night with her mom and her. Is it ok if I go?"

Sarah's mom was sure her daughter would be better off at her friend's house than she was moping around home alone. "Sure, sweetie. Just don't stay too late. Don't forget that you are going to be a working girl now."

Sarah drove her mom's Rover over to the Ward's and found Cassie waiting with a bowl of popcorn. "Want to watch 'Under the Tuscan Sun'? It's Mom's favorite movie."

Sarah's mood lifted from just being around her friend. "I'd love to watch one of my favorite movies." She took the bowl of popcorn, poured diet Mt. Dew over ice and settled into the couch, ready for the movie. She was so glad to have her friends and Cassie was the best. Unfortunately, Cassie would be leaving her for the summer too. But Cassie's mom reminded her that she had promised to help with the farm. It would be good to visit the Howard Farm. Sarah liked Leigh, Cassie's mom. She'd feel as if she was of value while waiting for the summer to be over.

When Sarah arrived home after the movie, her mom told her to take a day to rest between school and beginning her work with the Animal Clinic. Sarah didn't want the free time. It just gave her more time to miss Jake and Cassie. She asked her mom if she could come in after lunch just to get familiar with everything in the office. Joyce agreed. She was excited to have Sarah around and to have her daughter interested in her profession. She loved her job and thought Sarah would be a natural at it. "I'll leave the Rover for you to drive in tomorrow when you're ready to come down to the office."

"Thanks, Mom. Want to have lunch with your favorite daughter?" She asked.

"I'd love to have lunch with my favorite daughter and employee!" She squeezed Sarah's arm. "Now, it's time for the employer to find her bed. Tomorrow I have three farms to visit, and they are all on different ends of the county. I'll try to make it back to the office between visiting."

"Good night, Mom. I love you."

"I love you too, sweetie. Don't stay up late; you have a long day tomorrow."

Sarah felt the emptiness she had avoided all afternoon seep into the room. Oh Jake, why do we have to stay away from each other for so long? Now was the time that Jake and she would usually steal time for themselves. Her routine was to get ready for bed and snuggle in with her phone and talk with Jake for hours. But tonight she would climb into bed without talking to Jake. For the first time in years, they wouldn't talk to each other before going to sleep.

Joyce saw the dark cloud close in on her daughter. Sarah was struggling with Jake's absence and it hurt Joyce to see her distraught. The one thing Joyce could do was keep Sarah busy, and she planned to do so. Her strategy was that if Sarah was working, she wouldn't have time to think about how much she missed Jake. Plus, she had so much work to catch up on in the office that it was just a bit selfish of her to use her daughter to help out.

The next day, Sarah made it to the office around 12 noon, just in time for lunch with her mother. Joyce made it to the office only minutes after Sarah. Sarah brought KFC chicken, her mother's favorite. They went to the conference room to have lunch and to share mother-daughter time. These times were few and far between due to how busy each of them was. They both enjoyed talking about the animals and about what would be happening at the clinic during the summer.

Sarah was getting excited the more she spoke

with her mom. She began looking forward to the summer and working with the animals. She told her mom as much before Joyce left to visit Bloomington Branch. Joyce started out the door but hesitated, stopped and returned to give Sarah a hug.

NINE

By the end of the day, Sarah realized she had enjoyed her day at work and was looking forward to coming back tomorrow. But once she finished and began gathering her purse and keys to go home, she realized she had to face being alone. She would go home without Jake to discuss her day. This time of day was going to be the worst. She drove the Rover home slowly wondering what she would do for the entire evening. Her mom wouldn't be home until late, and her dad was in Campton buying cattle for the farm. When she drove into the driveway, she saw Heine in the pasture. Without thinking, Sarah found herself walking to the barn to do her chores. She missed having Jake there to help her. He always made her laugh. She missed their closeness during the evening routine of chores in the barn.

She found herself daydreaming about their laughs, kisses, hugs, caresses. She wondered what he was doing. Then she remembered. She looked at her watch to see that she only had ten minutes until 4 o'clock. She would start her thoughts of Jake early. She sent her thoughts of love to her boyfriend who was over a hundred miles away. "I miss you, Jake."

What to do until tomorrow morning? She found herself wandering around the house aimlessly. She decided to go over to Cassie's again. Her friend wouldn't be leaving until midweek. She wrote a note for her mom and off she went in the Rover. She drove up to Cassie's house and remembered she hadn't called first. She didn't know what Cassie had going on this evening. She and Josh could be busy. She decided to knock on the door, hoping her friend would be free.

Leigh, Cassie's mom, answered the door. She told Sarah that Cassie had gone to Josh's house, but she was welcome to go to the barns with her and help with the feeding. "If you have time we could discuss our plans for this summer."

Sarah was more than glad for the chance to be busy. She liked Cassie's mom. She made talking easy and comfortable. They discussed Cassie's visit to her dad's and Leigh's plans for the summer. Sarah realized that Cassie's mom was feeling some of the same feelings as she. They decided they would have to keep each other from being lonely for the ones they loved.

Leigh invited Sarah in for a snack, but Sarah told her that she needed to go home. Her mother would be home, and she wanted to spend some time with her. She told Leigh of the fun time she had while working at the clinic. Leigh was genuinely excited for Sarah and the town. "We need another vet in the county, Sarah."

Back home, Sarah noticed her mom's truck sitting in the drive. She rushed to the house calling "Mom!" as she entered. Her mom was resting in the living room and patted the seat next to her on the couch. Sarah went over and snuggled next to her mother. "I loved working at the clinic, Mom. Thank you for this opportunity."

Joyce hugged her daughter. "You are welcome, my little girl. And just think; you get to start early tomorrow and enjoy the work all day long. Maybe you can even go with me to Old Auntie Bea's tomorrow after work."

Sarah loved the old lady whom everyone called Old Auntie Bea. She was an older woman who had no living relatives, and so the townspeople had made her a member of all their families. Auntie Bea had a small farm on the outskirts of town. She had plenty of dogs and cats along with a few goats. Sarah's mom made a visit to check on her animals and Auntie Bea every few months. She was glad her mom had invited her to join her for the visit tomorrow. "I'd love to join you, Mom. Thanks, for inviting me."

The next morning Sarah was up and ready for work when her mom came down for her coffee. "Wow, look at you. Good morning."

"Good morning. I'm ready for work. Let's go. I have your coffee ready, and your bag is on the table. Let's get a move on, shall we?" Sarah giggled. She knew her mom was as slow as she during the morning.

Joyce grabbed her bag and coffee and motioned Sarah out the door. They made it to work early, and Joyce briefed Sarah on what she needed to work on for the day. She told her she would see her in the afternoon and was off to make her appointments.

Sarah began her tasks and quickly became engrossed in the work at hand. She had the opportunity to welcome several cats and dogs to the office and to watch as her mother's assistant checked out the animals. When her mom came rushing back, everyone became calm. She was so proud of her mother. She was excellent at her job, and everyone knew it. They all admired her for her professional work. Sarah wanted to be just like her mom. She laughed at herself. How corny, but true.

By the time her mom checked in at her office, Sarah had been knee deep in paperwork all morning and again in the afternoon. She would take a break to visit with the animals in the waiting room for a moment. She'd offer the pet owners coffee and the animal patients a small treat to satisfy their confinement with the other animals.

It was a noisy place. The conversation was always the same. Everyone had a story to tell about their animals and how they were special. Each animal was unique and yet when one looked at that particular dog or cat or hamster, it looked normal, almost like all the other dogs or cats or hamsters that populated the waiting room. Sarah amused herself with her thoughts. She guessed she was the same with her horses and her family cat Jasper. At any rate, she made it her job to make sure that the patients and their owners were as comfortable as possible while waiting to see the doctor or one of her interns.

When Joyce checked on the last patient, she found a silent waiting room and a pleasant surprise. Sarah had made a huge dent in the ever growing mound of paperwork. "Oh my goodness, Sarah; you are worth your weight in gold. Getting this paperwork filed is fantastic. Thank you for working so diligently." She laid her white coat across her arm and offered Sarah one of her own. Let's see what Auntie Bea is up to today. Shall we?"

When Sarah and her mother arrived, Old Auntie Bea was sitting on the front porch with cats and dogs surrounding her. At first glance, it looked as if Auntie Bea was having story time and the animals were gathering to listen. She was fanning herself with a section of the newspaper discarded days ago. When she saw Dr. Arnett pull up the driveway, her face lit up. She didn't have a lot of visitors, and she considered

Doc Arnett one of her friends. She slowly rose from her chair and walked to the front of the porch, being careful not to step on any animals' tails.

Sarah had known Auntie Bea her whole life. If a stranger saw this scene, they would come to the conclusion that Auntie Bea was insane and needed to be taken away from her home because she wasn't able to make good decisions. She knew this because a few years ago, that's what Social Services had tried to do. With the help of Sarah's mom and other well-known citizens of Salyersville, they fought for Auntie Bea and won. So now Auntie Bea lived in her home with her animals, and Sarah's mom came to visit to check on things.

Every opportunity Sarah had to join her mom's visits, she went. She loved talking with the old woman. Talking with Auntie Bea was similar to talking with Josh's Mammy, but Auntie Bea was more eccentric than Mammy. Like Mammy, Auntie Bea knew things about the town that no one else knew. She could tell stories about residents of Salyersville whom everyone had forgotten over the years.

Sarah noticed the time. It was 4 o'clock. It was

time to fulfill her promise to Jake. "Mom, can I meet you on the porch in a few minutes? There is something I have to do first."

Her mom grabbed her bag and glancing to the porch, absently muttered, "Take your time dear."

Sarah watched as her mom made her way through the cats' and dogs' tails to find Auntie Bea and gave her a big hug. She stopped watching her mom and Auntie Bea and began her ritual of thinking of Jake for a moment. "I miss you Jake, but you would be pleased with me. I am staying busy, and so far it hasn't been so bad. Not seeing you every day is bad, but I am keeping busy. The evenings are the worst. I catch myself looking and listening for you and the Chevy to come roaring to a stop, but you never do. Okay, I am not going to allow this to ruin my mood. I love you; please stay safe and true."

She jumped from the vet van and just as her mom had done, she moved slowly through the animal tails to Auntie Bea.

Auntie Bea was waiting for her hug. She always made Sarah feel special when she visited. She had served Joyce a glass of lemonade and offered Sarah a glass of her own. Sarah accepted although she knew that neither her mother nor she would be drinking it. She loved Auntie Bea, but she carried her practice of treating her cats and dogs as family a bit too far-- all the way into the kitchen. They didn't feel comfortable drinking out of her glassware.

While Auntie Bea was in the kitchen getting Sarah a glass of lemonade, Joyce poured half of her glass into the plant on the side of the porch. Sarah and Joyce giggled. They had not completely regained their composure when Auntie Bea came pushing the screen door open allowing three cats to find their way into the house and out of the hot sun on the porch.

Auntie Bea sat down beside the two and took a sip of her lemonade. She leaned forward as if needing to see their faces better and asked, "I hear we have new neighbors in town. Did strangers buy the Gamble Farm up your way?"

Sarah was surprised that Auntie Bea had heard about the new owners of Gamble Farm. She wondered what Bea knew about the Lazra family. When asked about what she had heard about the new owners Auntie

Bea shook her head. She didn't know anything more than Joyce or Sarah.

Auntie Bea was an expert on gossip. If the gossip was out there, she knew it and felt it her responsibility to inform all those she could think of the news. On this occasion, she didn't know a whole lot and pumped Joyce and Sarah for information. The only thing she could pull out of the two was Samuel's name. Sarah was only too happy to supply any details she could for Auntie Bea's stockpile of information to disperse to all who would listen.

On their way home, Joyce noted how late they would be getting home and decided takeout food was the answer for dinner. Her husband would be waiting for them when they got home. "Would you like Betty's Pizza, KFC or Lee's for dinner?"

Sarah pretended to be in deep thought over her choices for a few moments and then determined, "Lee's sounds great!" Joyce made her way into the drive through and ordered a huge box of chicken strips along with fries and coleslaw. Once they picked up the chicken, the aroma reminded her of how hungry she had gotten after her busy day of work.

She smiled to herself, another day to mark on the calendar and so far she was doing okay without her best friend and boyfriend hanging around. She wondered what Jake was doing at this moment. She didn't allow the old feeling of loneliness to stay for long. She had things to do. She ate dinner with her mom and dad, then rushed over to Cassie's to say goodbye. Cassie was leaving for her dad's in the morning.

Cassie was glad to see Sarah. Josh had been moping around all afternoon. He would obviously miss having Cassie around. Sarah gave him a friendly hug. "I know how you feel."

Cassie's mom wasn't in much of a better mood. She had a smile pasted on her face and tried to make her voice sound cheerful, but it just sounded shrill. Cassie gave Sarah one of her looks; a look that said, "Take care of my mom." Sarah shook her head agreeing to do just that. Although she had fleeting thoughts of the lady that haunted the house, she was looking forward to visiting with Leigh.

She decided to help Leigh think of something other than her daughter preparing to walk out the door for four weeks. "Leigh, would it be okay if I came over after work tomorrow and help out at the barn?"

Leigh smiled, "Of course, and why don't we get a couple of Blue Bonny ice creams and we'll watch a movie?"

Sarah smiled back, "I'd love to watch a movie tomorrow. Hey, have you seen the new Twilight movie? Maybe we could go this weekend."

Leigh agreed, "But I have to rent the first one before I go to see a sequel."

All three of the teenagers looked at Leigh. "You haven't seen or read any of the Twilight series?" Sarah queried.

Leigh feigning guilt admitted, "No, I haven't seen any of the movies or read the books. I know I need to get Cassie's books out and start reading."

Sarah volunteered, "Why don't I bring my copy of the first movie over tomorrow and you can watch it while I remind myself of the events from the first book again?"

Leigh agreed, "That sounds like a good plan. I

can't wait to have my second best girl spend an evening with me tomorrow."

Josh, looking miserable offered, "What about me? I'm going to be alone, too."

They all laughed at his sad mood. Cassie hugged him, "Oh, my poor, poor, poor boy. I'll call you every day, okay?"

He dropped his head and mumbled, "Okay."

TEN

The next day after work, Sarah decided that summer had lengthened the day's sunlight long enough that she could ride Heine over the ridge to Leigh's house. It wouldn't be dark until she returned after the movie. Heine was happy to be getting out of the pasture, and Sarah was happy to be riding him. She got him saddled and ready for their ride. As she mounted him and climbed the ridge, she wondered what to do about going past Gamble Farm. Did she dare take the easy route and pass by the property lines?

She had her cell phone if it held a signal while passing the Gamble Farm. If anything suspicious happened, she would be ready to call for help and flee. Besides, the last time the friends rode past there, the men were nowhere to be seen. Only Samuel came around. Seeing Samuel wouldn't be so bad, would it? She decided to take the short cut, passing by the Gamble Farm property line. It was summer; surely

Samuel's family found the sun helped with their cold moods.

Anyway, she was more than a little curious to see Samuel's family. She slowed Heine once she was close enough to see the Gamble's barns roofs. She tried to walk Heine quietly down the trail past the farm. She checked out the property line and didn't see any sign of the dark-clad men that were there before. Maybe the day they discovered them was a one-time thing and they wouldn't be around anymore. She sincerely hoped that to be the case.

Just as she began to breathe normally, she heard something coming from behind her. She quickened Heine's step. Whatever followed her, got quicker along with her.

She moved faster and again the footsteps behind her got faster. Her heart felt like it was trying to burst out of her chest. What should she do? What could be following her for so long without stopping? She just wanted to be home, safe. She rounded the bend and saw the Howard barns in the distance. If she could make it to the barns, maybe Leigh was waiting for her there and whatever was following her would go away.

She couldn't think any further ahead than that. She could hear the footsteps coming closer to her. She nudged Heine to go faster, and he obliged. She was going at top speed down the hill. She refused to go any faster in fear that Heine would be in danger of breaking a leg.

She made it down the hill and as she got closer to the barns she realized the footsteps had disappeared. Had the person or thing given up catching her? She finally glanced back to see what she could see. There was nothing except the woods and hills standing as far as she could see. She trotted Heine, giving him time to cool down and relax before going over to the barns.

Leigh was indeed in one of the barns doing the chores. Sarah apologized for being late but neglected to mention what had just happened to her. She didn't think anyone would believe her if she told them so she would just keep the incident to herself. Leigh looked up from the stall where she was putting clean straw and greeted Sarah. "Hey, it's good to see you."

Sarah smiled and tested her voice, "You've almost finished. Am I late?"

Leigh replied, "Oh no, I just wanted to have more time to spend with you during our movie date. Did you bring the movie?"

Sarah reached into her sack and plucked out the movie. "We're ready."

Leigh finished the stall she was working on and announced, "That's it. We're ready. Let the movie begin." She grabbed Sarah's arm and led her across the road to the house.

Sarah enjoyed the evening with Leigh although the thoughts of her experience near the Gamble Farm sent chills down her spine. She was tempted to ask Leigh to drive her back home but knew she had Heine. She had to get him home tonight.

Once the movie was over she bid Leigh goodbye; noting that the sun was going down soon, and she didn't want to be out riding in the darkness of the night. Luckily, Leigh didn't question her although she must have realized that Sarah and Cassie had been riding at night several times before tonight. Sarah was glad and said her goodbyes once again and got Heine ready for their trip back home. She could feel her heart quickening when she mounted her beautiful horse. "Let's go, boy."

She moved slowly up the hill and around the ridge to the Gamble Farm. So far nothing out of the ordinary had occurred. Was she crazy and just imagined that something had been coming after her? Whatever the answer, she hoped it stayed away and she made it home soon.

Sarah began allowing herself to breathe once she got to the other end of the Gamble Farm. She was almost on her family's land. She began thinking of Jake, and realized that their first week apart was more than half over. Then, without warning, her thoughts of Jake were interrupted with the pounding of what must be feet. She held back a scream and pushed in on Heine's flanks. He quickened his pace, alert to his owner's tension. She concentrated on her path, trying not to think of what was coming up behind her. The quicker she and Heine moved, the quicker the footsteps got. She wasn't going to run faster than the thing this time. She was doomed. She galloped past the fence row of her farm hoping whatever was following would stay on the Gamble Farm. It did not. She could still hear the footsteps coming even closer behind Heine and her. She steadied her nerves and willed herself to stop and turn to face her attacker. What she saw startled both her pursuer and her.

There, riding behind her was Samuel on his beautiful white horse. She wanted to scream "Why?" But she decided to hide her frustration. She steadied her voice and without showing any emotion, asked, "What are you doing around here Samuel?"

In typical Samuel fashion, he answered, "I could ask you the same thing, Sarah." He seemed to be studying her. It was as if she was the intruder instead of him.

"I live here Samuel. I travel these hills regularly." She stared him down. He had scared her to an inch of her life. She was angry enough to give back as much as he gave her. She was sure she saw a flicker of a smile lurking under his frozen, perfect facial features.

"And I could say the same, Sarah. I live here also, and I plan to travel these hills on a regular basis myself." He stared back at her. It was like playing chess, and Sarah was sure Samuel was the type to be able to beat her at chess any day of the week. She gave in to him.

"Touché," she shrieked. She hadn't meant for her voice to be shrill, but her nerves were on edge and hard to control at the moment. "You do live here with all of us Buffaloers, don't you? I forget about the Lazra's since we don't see them around town. As a matter of fact, you are the only Lazra I have seen since you moved onto Gamble Farm. Oh, except for all those men who must have been your relatives helping get you situated." She faked innocence. She knew what she was doing. She didn't know much about Samuel, but the one thing she had learned was that he couldn't handle discussing his family.

Sarah watched as Samuel visually shut down. He pulled his expressionless face into place and quickly bid her a polite goodbye as he led his horse back toward Gamble Farm. Sarah began to breathe normally again. Samuel had reacted the way Sarah had expected. The daylight was getting dusky, and she needed to get back home. Her parents would worry if she was out alone after dark. She rode her horse off the hill and to the barn where she found her dad unloading the new herd of cattle he had purchased.

"Hi, Sarah, how is my favorite gal?" he asked, as he slammed the stall door on the last cow. He turned to check on his daughter when he heard her voice. "You sound angry, honey. What happened to get you in a mood? Is your mom a slave driver at work?" His eyes danced.

Sarah giggled, her mood lightened quickly, "No, she is the best boss, ever."

Her father frowned, "I won't be telling her you said that. We need to keep her on her toes. Give me some dirt on the woman. Help me out a little." He faked a plea.

Sarah disturbed the livestock with her deep laugh. She hadn't laughed that hard since Jake had left. Her parents were so in love -- still. She hoped she and Jake could keep their relationship as romantic as her parents. She grabbed her dad's hand and led him from the barn toward the house where her mother waited for them both. When they entered the house, Joyce came from the living room hugging Sarah first and then sharing a long lingering hug with her husband of twenty years.

Sarah smiled and made an excuse of washing her hair tonight so she could sleep in tomorrow morning. She wanted to give them some alone time, and they did not argue. She slipped away upstairs and to her room where her thoughts filled with Samuel. Who was this person that kept showing up, keeping her tense and anxious? Why was she always upset with him? She couldn't put her finger on the answer to that one. She wished Jake was there; she would call him and vent to him. He would listen and then tell her she was overreacting. "Stay still and it will work itself out," she heard him saying.

"Okay, I'll try," she replied to her mind's vision of Jake. She went to bed and said goodnight to Jake and Cassie, turned to her side and waited for sleep.

ELEVEN

The next week Josh called Sarah. He wanted her to come over to his farm and go with him to visit Mammy. "It's been a while since we all went for a visit, and I think she's lonely. She was asking about the gang and since we're the only ones around I thought we'd go for a visit."

Sarah eagerly agreed to meet him at Cassie's barn. Josh suggested they take the horses out for a ride.

"I'd love to visit Mammy. And you know how lonely it's been around here without having everyone around all the time." Sarah looked at her phone as if she could impress on Josh just how much she missed Jake.

"I know what you mean. I can't wait until Cassie gets home from Louisville. At least we can talk every night. You can't even have a conversation with Jake. That has to be horrible." He listened to the silence on the other end of the phone and realized Sarah was having a much harder time than he imagined. "Let's enjoy the day tomorrow, shall we? You know both Cassie and Jake want us to have a good summer." They planned to meet right after work the next day.

Sarah left work early so that she could get Heine ready for the ride. She wasn't anxious to ride by the Gamble Farm again but refused to give Samuel the power to influence her decisions. She would ride on her usual route that she had always ridden. Of course, she would stay clear of the Gamble property, but she refused to be bullied off the trail to her best friend's house.

She mounted Heine and up the hill they went. Sarah swallowed her fear and was brave until she hit the ridge behind the Gamble Farm, and she realized her lungs were still. It was as if her body had decided that if she breathed, she would disturb the farm, and she would be in trouble. She was angry with herself for allowing Samuel to make her feel this way about her home. She kept riding past the Lazra's and began to breathe as she made her descent down the hill toward Cassie's barns. She felt the heaviness of fear and dread leave her body, as she got closer to the barns.

She was elated to see Josh standing at the entrance of the barn. "Hey, Sarah, want to visit a wonderful lady and maybe have a snack?" Josh asked as he smacked his lips in anticipation of Mammy's good cooking.

"I'd like nothing better than to spend the evening with Mammy," she declared. "How are you, Josh?" She pulled a serious face.

He made one back at her, "I'm doing okay. I'm trying to keep busy on the farm, and to be honest; it isn't hard. There is so much work to do there during the summer months. Dad is grateful that I'm so willing to work all the time," he laughed. "How are you doing without Jake around?"

Sarah thought about it for a moment and responded, "I'm doing okay. I'm working with mom at the clinic and staying busy, too. It's easier than I thought it would be, I guess."

He led his horse, Wildfire, out of the barn and pulled himself on its back. "Let's ride, shall we?"

Sarah nudged Heine and off she ran in front of Josh. "Hey, that is not fair." he yelled as he pushed Wildfire to race past Sarah.

They galloped the whole way to Mammy's and didn't stop until Mammy opened the door laughing at the two as they foot raced into her house and to the kitchen.

They knew Mammy would have good food ready for them, and she didn't disappoint. The dining table held fried chicken and potato salad with cornbread. The desserts consisted of lemon meringue pie, apple pie, peach cobbler, and banana pudding. Josh allowed the air to leave his chest. He made a low growl that sounded like a caveman going in for the kill. Mammy and Sarah laughed, and Sarah found her seat beside Josh. He didn't wait for her to begin eating, he was already taking large portions of food from the serving dishes on the table. Mammy's face was full of joy. She lived to have her great-grandson and his friends enjoy her food.

Mammy took a moment to ask Sarah, "How are you doing this summer, Sarah? Are you doing anything exciting while you're off from school?"

"I'm doing fine, Mammy. I'm working with my mom at her veterinarian practice. Working at the clinic is exciting. I want to follow in her footsteps and hopefully, work with her someday." Sarah surprised herself with her honesty about her plans. She hadn't discussed her wish to join her mom in her practice with anyone. Although, she knew her mother would be thrilled if she decided to work with her.

"I am very proud of you kids. You're mature and level headed. You keep your dreams with you and make your mind up to let nothing get in your way."

Sarah smiled, "I'll try my best, Mammy."

Mammy then turned to Josh and asked, "Josh, have you heard any more about the family that bought the Gamble place?"

Josh took a drink of milk to wash down some of the food he had stuffed in his mouth and replied, "No, ma'am, I've been close to home this summer helping Dad every day. I haven't had time to ask around. Sarah, have you found out any more about Samuel since school ended?"

Sarah shook her head no. She didn't want to

explain her meetings with Samuel. She wasn't sure why she cared. She was going to assume that she just didn't want to get angry again. Thinking of their meetings made her remember that she had to go past his farm to get home. She looked at Josh and asked, "Josh, can we go soon? I hate being out on the trail after dark."

Josh finished the last bite of lemon meringue pie and got up from the table. He strolled over to Mammy and gave her the biggest hug and kiss. She beamed. Sarah got up from her seat and hugged Mammy and pecked her cheek.

Mammy begged, "Will you two come back by and keep me company again? Since your friends are out of town, you can make time pass with me."

They both looked at each other and then at Mammy and agreed. "We'll be here if you supply some more of your good cooking." Josh toyed.

Sarah nodded her head in agreement. Mammy asked for their request for next time. Josh quickly gave her a list of dishes he had been craving as Sarah nodded in agreement.

"Does next week, say Wednesday, sound okay?" Mammy asked.

"Perfect!" they both cried. "See you next week, Mammy," Josh yelled. He remembered the race with Sarah and ran out of the room with Sarah chasing after him once she realized the race was on. Mammy's wrinkled body jiggled with laughter.

Off they galloped toward Josh's farm. Sarah stopped in front of the barn and told Josh she would be fine to ride home from his house. He offered to ride with her, but she refused to be paranoid about the trail. She made good time until she came up to the ridge around the Gamble Farm and then she felt the fear settle in her bones. She rode silently down the trail until she saw the white horse once again standing in wait for her. She wondered if he had seen her pass by earlier and had camped out on the trail in wait. She forced herself to put a smile on her face as she neared Samuel.

"Sarah, I need to talk with you. May I ride with you for a while on your way home?" Sarah looked at Samuel's face and saw only the seriousness that was usual for him.

"Why would you want to ride with me? It isn't like you have been putting forth any effort to spend time with us before now." She knew she sounded snooty, but she didn't care.

Samuel rode close to Heine and whispered, "It is important that I spend time with you. Please allow me to ride with you." His intense request had her alarmed.

"Okay, that will be all right." Sarah searched his face for the missing information he was not sharing, but only saw something that made her feel alarmed. She couldn't decide what emotion his face displayed, but it wasn't good.

He pulled his horse close to Heine, and they moved down the trail slowly. Once they were out of site of his property he grabbed Heine's rein and stopped.

"Sarah, I fear for you to travel this trail. It may not be safe for you. I will protect you as much as I can, but if I am not around, and you decide to visit, it could be a catastrophe for you and your friends."

Sarah searched his face. "What are you talking

about, Samuel? What kind of trouble can we get into for just traveling a trail that doesn't even touch your property?" What she saw was a boy that was distressed. For a moment, she felt sorry for him. She felt Samuel was trapped in this world, and she couldn't help him. "I am sorry, Samuel, but your family can't rob us of our childhood stomping ground. Why do they care that we ride over these hills?"

Samuel came closer to her and touched her hand. "Please trust me and listen to me. Please don't ride around the ridge anymore. There has to be another route you can take that isn't near our land that will be safer." His eyes pleaded with her.

Samuel looked at Sarah for a long time. Finally, he asked, "Sarah, could you invite me over to your house, and I'll try to explain as much as I can?" He looked urgently into her eyes. She was confused and disoriented. Samuel's demand was too much for her to wrap her brain around. She shook her head yes. He looked deep into her eyes, "Will tomorrow at 4 o'clock be okay?"

She shook her head okay, but then remembered Jake. She quickly grabbed his hand and shook her head in a very pronounced "no". "You can't come over until 5 o'clock," she almost screamed. He relented and agreed with a nod of his head. He removed his hand from under Sarah's and looked up the hill as if a ghost were watching. He leaned over and kissed her hand. Sarah slipped her hand away and looked questioningly at Samuel.

Samuel's face was as usual void of emotion except for his eyes. She noted that his eyes gave way to what she believed was fear. He explained, "You'll understand more tomorrow once we talk." She nodded and turned Heine away from Samuel and toward home. She moved over the trail back to her barn slowly, while trying to decipher what just happened. If he had been trying to make her feel protected, he failed terribly. She was anxious to hear more tomorrow.

Once she finished taking care of Heine, she went to the house and found her mother. "Mom, I think our new neighbor just invited himself to our house tomorrow at 5 o'clock. Is that okay?" Sarah's mom stopped working on her computer to stare at her daughter.

"Are you sure you want to have another boy to

the house while Jake is gone?" She searched Sarah's face for an explanation. She found nothing --just an anguished look on her daughter's face.

Sarah faked busyness and mumbled, "I'm just acting as a friend to someone who is new to the neighborhood. It's nothing more." She allowed her eyes to find her mother and smiled what she hoped was a convincing smile.

"Of course, he can come over, Sarah. I'd like to learn more about our new neighbors."

Sarah grumbled, "Good luck with that. Will you stay close, Mom?"

"Of course, I will stay close, and your dad will be here, too," her mom assured.

Sarah went to her room still in a daze. She went to bed and instead of thinking about Jake, she could think only of Samuel and his panic-stricken face. She had never felt so uncomfortable in her neighborhood before this. She didn't like it at all.

TWELVE

At 4 o'clock the next day, Sarah found herself thinking of Jake. She wished he were here to meet with Samuel this afternoon. Her parents had both ended up with business to take care of before they could join Samuel and her, leaving her alone to host the new neighbor for a while. She had to admit that she was dreading the evening. She was curious, but if she was honest, more than a little scared of what Samuel had to say. They all thought that something odd was happening on the Gamble Farm, but no one could put their finger on what was wrong with the situation.

Even Auntie Bea and Mammy had been dumbfounded when given the facts. Hopefully, Samuel would give her some information to help solve the mystery about their new neighbors.

She shook her head in an attempt to free her mind from Samuel and the strangeness he had brought to her life. This was her time to think of Jake, and here she was thinking of Samuel and his family. She refused to allow Samuel to take Jake's time. "I love you, Jake. Come home soon." She rushed inside her house at 4:45 and went upstairs to make sure she was presentable.

At 5 o'clock precisely the doorbell rang. Of course, Samuel would be punctual to a fault. She rushed downstairs to answer the door. Her mom was called to one of the farms in Morgan County to deliver a foal, which meant she would be late in the evening getting home, even if the foal was okay. That left her alone to deal with Samuel. Her dad wouldn't be home until around 7:00 if he was successful on his buying trip.

"Hi, Samuel, won't you come in?" She led him into the living room and sat on the couch; the couch she and Jake shared while watching TV or making out. She felt guilty having another boy sitting on their sofa.

Samuel looked flustered, a first for him. He didn't display his controlled composure for once. Sarah had begun to consider this quality one of his shortcomings. But after taking a good look at him she was concerned for him. "Are you alright, Samuel?

You look stressed."

Like a light switch, Samuel changed his expression and the way he held himself. Once again he was the handsome, reserved boy who gave nothing away. He graciously took a seat beside Sarah and smiled the cold, reserved smile she was used to seeing. She became angry. He was the one that asked, no begged, for this meeting and now he was acting as if he was doing her a favor just gracing her with his presence. The nerve of this guy.

She pierced his eyes with her own. "Are you for real? What is going on with you, Samuel? Why are you demanding that my friends and I stay away from the trail? You know we don't and won't trespass on your precious land."

She glared at him, waiting for answers. Samuel looked into Sarah's eyes. She wasn't prepared for what she saw. Panic was written all over his face. "Sarah, believe me, I don't want to be here to tell you what I have to say any more than you want me to." When Sarah opened her mouth to protest, Samuel held up his hand, stopping her.

"I have to say this, or I can't live with myself. Whether you believe it or not, I like your friends and you very much. That is why I have been staying close to the trail. I want to protect you if I can. I am just not sure how much longer I will or can be successful." He turned his body toward Sarah and leaned close, "Tell me you will not travel the trail next to the property? You can persuade your friends to stay away; they'll listen to you."

Sarah looked back at Samuel; suspicion draped her face. "Why should I do this just because someone I have only met and know absolutely nothing about has requested me to do so? For all I know, you bought your farm as a façade for your family's illegal activities. Let's face it, a stranger from Connecticut buys a farm in the middle of nowhere and says he wants to be a part of the community, but his family won't show their faces. I mean, your relatives didn't look like they were farmers if you know what I mean."

Samuel didn't flinch from her wrath. He stared back at her without blinking. "Sarah, I cannot tell you the details you want to know. It would be unhealthy for you and me if you knew anything other than what

I am telling you right now."

Sarah shook her head as if shaking free from the confusion she was feeling toward Samuel. "What are you talking about, Samuel? You act like your family is the MOB or CIA agents or vampires, or something. Surely you are overreacting to something they have said. Are they going to try to get the law to prevent us from riding the four-wheelers too close to the house? I'll make sure we don't ride anywhere near the house, okay?"

Samuel lost his reserve, and the panic rushed back. "You guys have to stay away for your safety. No more traveling the trail on four-wheelers, horses, foot, roller skates, whatever your mode of travel might be-- you have to stay away. Please, Sarah, listen to me." He had completely lost his cold exterior and was shouting at Sarah.

She felt scared and just as she came to herself and began to stand; Samuel grabbed her hand and pulled her back to the seat. He caressed her arm and moved her close to him. "I'm sorry, Sarah. I'm so sorry to scare you. Please forgive me."

In the middle of this unreal dream she was living in, she smelled his scent. He smelled good, and his chest was firm and solid. She felt protected resting next to him. She reluctantly pulled her head up to look at Samuel's face. She saw tears sliding down his cheek. He moved his hand to her face and wiped away the tears she didn't realize she had shed. She didn't know why they both were crying but it seemed appropriate for what was happening. The memory of Jake was far away while she did the same to his. With all that had just happened, it felt right. She would be mortified later, once the moment passed.

They sat on the couch in her living room in silence for a long moment or maybe not so long. Sarah wasn't sure. Maybe this was just a dream, and she would wake to find morning and be in a rush to get to work. Samuel was the first to move. "Sarah, I have to go. Promise me you won't travel close to the property." He searched her face for the promise.

She looked back at his concerned face and agreed, "I promise I won't travel close to Gamble Farm, and I will try my best to keep my friends away."

Samuel's face was almost angry. "No, Sarah,

you must keep them safe. Keep them away from the farm. Do you hear me?"

Sarah became alarmed again, "I will, Samuel, I will!"

His face relaxed. "Then, I will go and leave you alone. I'm so sorry I had to do this to you and your friends, Sarah." He walked to the door, and as he stepped outside, he turned and smiled a genuine smile. "Except for the crap I had to bring to you, I have enjoyed myself tremendously. Thank you for your hospitality." Then, he was gone.

Sarah stood next to the couch. The couch where she had just leaned against Samuel crying with him. The couch where she and Jake used to lounge around. Her mind was whirling. Sarah felt like she was living in a nightmare. She felt as if her life was spiraling out of control and she couldn't stop it. She found herself reliving her conversation with Samuel. When she couldn't take thinking about Samuel and the situation, she would pace the room. She ended up standing by the couch, staring at the spot Samuel had occupied. Maybe if she stared long enough and tried hard enough, this nightmare would end. After all, there wasn't any evidence that Samuel was telling the truth. For reasons she couldn't explain she did believe him. His emotions were too strong to ignore. Standing by the couch is where her father found her.

"Hi, darling; how was your day? Your mom said you had company, where is he?"

Sarah shook her head to clear it and absently told her dad that Samuel had left a few minutes ago.

Her father's face revealed his disappointment. "I was hoping I would make it home in time to ask him about his family. I'd like to invite them to dinner. If we don't extend a warm welcome to them soon, they're going to think our little neighborhood is unfriendly."

"Why don't you let me ask Samuel, Dad? I'll ask him the next time our paths cross."

Her dad looked at her, "Okay. Are you and Samuel becoming good friends?"

Sarah snorted, "I wouldn't say that exactly."

Her dad took a good long look at her and then asked, "Have you talked with Jake's parents? Wonder if they have heard from him?"

Sarah's face drew into a sad pout, "No one can hear from him until he gets to come home. Although his parents get to visit once, Jake asked that they not make the trip since he would be home soon after the scheduled visitation." She dropped her eyes, shading her anxiety, "I don't want to think of how much longer we have to wait to see him."

Her dad came over and hugged her against his chest. Similar to the way Samuel had pulled her to him, she reminded herself. "He will be home soon, pumpkin. This time will pass, and Jake will be so much closer to his dream."

Sarah smiled, "I know, I know. It hasn't been as bad as I had dreaded."

At that moment, Sarah's mom rushed in the house. She stopped dead in her tracks. "He's gone already? I was going to ask him to invite his family to dinner." Sarah and her father looked at each other and then at her mom and burst into laughter.

THIRTEEN

The next morning, Sarah was busy working in the records room of the clinic when Becky, one of the receptionists burst into the room. Sarah was startled by Becky's heightened display of urgency. "Becky, are you okay?" Sarah looked at Becky's flushed face searching for a clue to explain why she was in turmoil.

Becky took a deep breath and slowly began telling Sarah the information she was intent on relaying, "Sarah, there is a handsome young man in our waiting room, and he's asking to see you." She gulped and took another deep breath. Her face was just as flushed as she was when she came in, but she was gaining control over her excitement. "Do you know who he is, Sarah? He's so far above HOT that I cannot think of words to describe him." Becky giggled and used her hand to exaggerate fanning her face and neck.

Sarah's heart began beating faster. Could it be

Samuel? He was the only person she could think of who the clinic staff wouldn't know. The rest of her friends had all been regular visitors throughout the years. She shook her head mostly to herself instead of Becky. Would Samuel come to her work to bother her with his families' trouble? Sarah felt the heat from her temper rise. She didn't want to play anymore. "Did he give you his name, Becky?"

Becky shook her head no, "I forgot to ask. I'm sorry."

Sarah couldn't resist laughing; Becky was acting silly. "It's okay, Becky. I think I know who might be visiting."

Sarah pulled her lab jacket back on and walked to the front desk. She prepared herself to see Samuel, and she wasn't disappointed. Great, she was getting another chance to listen to his dark and gloomy description of life on Buffalo Creek since he had moved in and messed up her life.

She looked at Samuel and smiled a plastered smile. She asked him to follow her to one of the empty exam rooms. Once she was in the room, and Samuel had followed, she shut the door. She turned to face him and didn't hold back any of her annoyance. "What can I do for you, Samuel? Last night wasn't enough?"

Samuel looked down at Sarah. He was visibly distressed. "Sarah, I am sorry, but I have no other choice than to visit you today." He looked pleadingly at Sarah. "I am going to ask you to go out with me, and I need you to … you need to … agree to go with me."

Sarah's mouth flew open. "Are you for real? In case you didn't notice while stalking my friends and me, I have a boyfriend that I really, really like." She looked glaringly at Samuel. "I can't believe your audacity these past few days. I mean, really, Samuel?"

He looked embarrassed, "I am truly sorry Sarah. I am trying to keep you and your friends safe. You must believe me."

Sarah exploded, "Why do I have to believe you? What have you done or said that would make me believe you? I have seen no reason I should trust you. You are someone that I just recently met, and I am supposed to believe you???

Samuel walked the few steps between the two

of them and grabbed Sarah's shoulders. "Sarah you know I am telling you the truth. Listen to me. We need to present a façade of more than friendship. It will be good for you and, alas, for me, also."

Sarah couldn't explain it, but she did believe Samuel. But believing him didn't make her like what was happening. His touch on her shoulders made her uncomfortable. Not because she didn't like it but because she did enjoy his touch --- too much. She must remember Jake during this ordeal. Oh, if only he were here. What was she to do? She did not want anyone to get the wrong idea; yet, Samuel was saying she needed to allow the wrong idea to spread. Sarah couldn't imagine why she and Samuel together would be safe? Samuel's expressionless face took on a fear that left him white and trembling. Sarah was surprised by Samuel's obvious distress. Whatever Samuel was fighting was real. She had no doubts. No one could act as scared as Samuel's face. The fear that engulfed him made her quickly relent to his request.

"So what do you suggest, Samuel?" She stared at his face waiting. She made herself step back away from the closeness of his body. Becky was right, he was handsome, and his body was too much to ignore. She thought, "Jake, where are you? Please hurry and come home."

Samuel, aware of Sarah's pulling away, stepped back a few steps himself. "I need to take you to dinner in town or do something you guys do for fun. Do you have any suggestions?"

Sarah's face became stubborn. "You know that I am going to tell Jake every detail of this when he returns."

Samuel smiled, "Of course."

Sarah settled into deep thought and after a few minutes her face lit up. "I know where we can go. Let's ride our horses over to my friend Cassie's farm and visit with her mother. That way you can get to know your next-door neighbor, and I can get away with being with you, and the date will only be a friend introducing a friend to another friend. What do you think?"

"I think I can make that work. Where will I pick you up and what time would be convenient for you?" He sounded like he was making a business deal with her. Sarah caught his dismissal of riding their horses over to the Howard farm. She reasoned that he didn't want them on the trail next to the Gamble farm for whatever reason. She would oblige him this time.

He saw the look on her face and smiled. Not the pasted on one that he used most of the time, but a genuine smile. "Thank you, Ms. Arnett, for allowing me to escort you to a … what kind of party can we say that we are attending?"

Sarah thought, "We all love to play Rook and have gatherings at our different houses. How about a Rook party?"

Samuel looked puzzled. "What is Rook?"

Sarah giggled in spite of herself. "It's a card game." She wrinkled her nose. "You've never played Rook?"

Samuel smiled his genuine smile and declared, "I don't think I've ever heard of it let alone played it."

Sarah nodded, "Then it's settled. I'll arrange it with Leigh to meet at her house, and I'll ask Josh to join us, too. That will make enough for Rook partners.

Get ready my friend; you are going to be a Rook playing fool before this night is over."

Surprisingly, Samuel laughed, "Okay, I can't wait to be made a fool." They both laughed at their jokes. "Pick you up at your house at 6 o'clock?"

"Call me tomorrow after lunch. That should give me time to ask Leigh if we can have a Rook game at her house tomorrow night." Sarah added.

Sarah wasn't surprised when Leigh agreed to have a Rook party for their new neighbor. As a matter of fact, Leigh was excited about the gathering. She was feeling lonely without Cassie in the house. She asked if Sarah would mind if Mark came over to play. Sarah agreed. She couldn't believe she hadn't thought about Mark from the beginning. Mark and Leigh had become very close in the past year. They had been high school sweethearts, and now two decades later, they had found each other again. They were the cutest couple she knew except for her parents, of course.

Sarah asked if she could invite Josh and maybe she could get Seth and Isabelle to come. Leigh was good with as many as Sarah wanted to invite.

When Samuel called, Sarah had good news. He asked if he could pick her up at her house, and she relented and said he could. Sarah was still unsure about Samuel's picking her up, but she would explain everything to Jake once he was home.

At 6 o'clock Samuel's red BMW pulled into her driveway. He was prompt as usual. Sarah answered the doorbell and grabbed her bag of goodies along with a deck of Rook cards. Samuel placed his hand on the small of her back and guided her to his car. He opened the door, and she climbed in and waited for him to find his way to the driver's side. Once he had his seatbelt on he turned to her and thanked her again for going with him. Sarah thought he leaned close to her --- just a smidge too close. Almost as if he was trying to make people believe that they were ready to kiss.

"If you're trying to make it look like we are on a real date; my parents won't believe that I'm going to cheat on Jake."

"I'm not worried about your parents, Sarah. Would you look into my eyes and touch my face with your hand?" He gazed into her eyes as if smitten with her. "Do it, Sarah. Please."

Sarah reached her hand to his hair to place a lock of his hair back into place. She was scared. What had she gotten herself into with Samuel? She slowly pulled her hand down to his cheek and allowed it to rest while staring back into his beautiful eyes.

"Good, Sarah." He pulled back to his side of the car and started the motor; away they moved to the highway. In moments, they were sitting in front of Cassie's house. He held her hand and motioned for her to stay seated.

He moved from the driver's seat and found Sarah's side of the car. He gently helped her from the car and guided her up the walk to the large porch. Sarah knocked on the door. Mark opened and waved them into the house. Josh was already sitting with Leigh on the couch, chomping on a bowl of popcorn. He looked up when Sarah and Samuel came into the living room. "Hey Sarah, how's it going?" Without waiting for an answer, he turned to Samuel offering his hand. "Good to see you, neighbor. Glad you decided to join us tonight."

Samuel shook Josh's hand and turned to thank Leigh for her invitation. Leigh welcomed him and asked him to tell his parents she was anxious to invite them to dinner. "I seem to keep missing them. I haven't met them yet."

Samuel smiled his pasted-on smile and agreed to relay her message. Mark followed them into the living room and offered Samuel his hand. While Samuel accepted Mark's welcome, Josh moved toward the dining room table. They all followed.

The huge antique buffet table that had belonged to Leigh's great-grandmother sat in the corner of the room heavy with all kinds of finger food. Sarah pulled her cake pops from the sack Samuel had carried for her and placed them on the buffet table. "Wow, Leigh you have outdone yourself with the food." The running joke at Leigh's house was that she only cooked from a box.

"It's amazing what you can find that is ready to be zapped in the microwave from a box anymore." They all laughed, and Leigh faked a what-are-you-laughing-at look at them all. She offered Samuel the pick of the table, and he graciously filled his plate with all sorts of sweets. It looked like stuffy; formal Samuel had a severe sweet tooth.

Sarah and Josh pushed and shoved each other trying to interfere with their masterpiece plates. Leigh and Mark waited until the young people finished, and they took their time talking and staring at each other while filling their plates. Once finished, they found their way to the table.

Mark sat on one end of the table and Leigh on the other end. Sarah asked Josh to be her partner so Samuel could observe the game being played and could learn how to play. "Sure, I'll be your partner. Just understand, Samuel, it takes a while to get as good as I am in Rook."

Samuel let his guard down, and Sarah heard a sweet laugh that she had never heard before now. He had a pleasant laugh once he allowed himself the pleasure of laughing. She smiled at his lapse of control. He was just a cute boy when he wasn't so tense.

Samuel sat next to Sarah while she explained the cards she played, what made for a good hand, and why she bid on particular cards. He studied her cards and nodded his head in understanding. Sarah and Josh had won that game; then Mark invited Samuel to take his place as Leigh's partner. Samuel accepted, and Sarah and Josh discovered that Samuel was a quick learner.

Sarah giggled when Josh came to attention after Samuel caught his black fourteen. By the end of the game, Sarah and Josh were wondering if they would pull out a win or not. The last hand helped to bring their win, and Leigh congratulated Samuel in learning so quickly. He smiled his genuine smile and offered Mark his spot back. Leigh begged off this game and gave her seat to Mark.

Josh moaned; he knew that Mark was on his throne, and he would make it hurt if a newbie helped to take it away from Josh. The game ended with Sarah and Josh the victors once again. Josh was getting cocky, and the others began planning on how to take Josh down and of course Sarah with him. Mark and Leigh played them again and this time, Josh and Sarah didn't have a chance. They played until 11 o'clock then Sarah reminded everyone she had to be home by midnight. She was a working girl nowadays.

They played one more game and then called it even since everyone had been sitting in the winner's seats at one time or another. Sarah asked Leigh about Cassie as she was gathering her things, and Samuel took them from her to carry to the car and thanked Leigh for her hospitality. Josh looked at Sarah quizzically. Sarah pretended not to notice.

"Josh, have you heard anything from Jake? I know you boys have your ways. I'm hoping he will attempt to contact one of you."

Josh gave Sarah a long asking look. "No, I don't think Jake would do anything to mess up this opportunity. He has wanted this for so long."

Sarah returned his long look. "I am so proud of him, and I can't wait to tell him when he gets back. Once this is over, and things are back to normal, I'll be glad he did it too." She hoped that was enough to allow Josh to understand that she was still Jake's.

Josh offered, "Sarah do you want me to run you home?"

Samuel stepped forward, "That's okay. I live just up the road. I'll drop Sarah off on my way home." He turned toward Sarah, "If that is okay with you, Sarah?"

"Sure, you boys can fight over who can serve me while Jake is away. Poor me," she giggled. Then she turned toward Josh. "Thanks, Josh, but Samuel is right. He is going right past my house, and he does have a BMW."

Everyone laughed, and Josh gave up, "I've been trumped," he declared.

Samuel guessed that her friends would be watching from the windows as they walked to the car, so he made his small load of Sarah's food seem like a lot for him to carry. Sarah was aware that he was making excuses on why he didn't have his arms around her. She was thankful that he considered her feelings during the situation. He opened her car door. She slid into the passenger side and waited for him to come to the driver's side. It took him a long time to find his way around the car. Once he sat down, he turned the car on and pulled out of the drive. He looked over at Sarah, "I need to kiss you before you leave the car, Sarah."

Sarah could not believe her ears. "Are you insane? No, you cannot kiss me. I have a boyfriend that I care for a whole lot."

Samuel looked at her and pulled her hand near his mouth. "I must show all those watching that you are very important to me. Please, Sarah." He placed a gentle kiss on the back of her hand and then turned her hand over and kissed the palm as well. He was tender. Sarah just sat and watched. She felt as if she was watching a Lifetime movie.

She looked over at him. She leaned closer to him. She told herself she was playing a part in a play with him. "Okay, but you know I love Jake." He shook his head and held her hand next to his face as he drove. Numb from this nightmare she was living, Sarah held her breath hoping that this craziness would soon end, and she could tell Jake all the details without any guilt.

"Will you look at me while I drive as if you can't get enough of me?" Samuel asked. Sarah had to laugh at his expression. "Or laugh while you are having such a good time with me," Samuel laughed, and Sarah felt that it was his real laugh not for the audience he insisted they had.

He pulled her up to her driveway and pulled her close. "I'm going to do it now, okay."

Sarah had never had anyone ask permission to plant a kiss before. "Okay," she whispered.

Samuel leaned over her and his lips gently caressed hers. They were soft and tender. His kiss was long and lingering. Sarah couldn't think of anything except the lips that felt so good on her own. The connection she felt was not from an act in a play. Did Samuel feel the same connection as she? She guessed that the answer was probably not. As good as he looked, he had surely kissed many girls in his life. She just wasn't used to anybody but Jake kissing her. Jake, Oh Jake, I'm so sorry.

Samuel regained his composure and pulled away from Sarah. He was as flustered as Sarah. "I'm sorry, Sarah. I got carried away. You're a good kisser." He ran his finger across her lips, and she couldn't help wondering if that was for their audience or did he mean this gesture.

She snapped her mind back to the situation at hand. Her voice still shaking, she breathed, "You aren't bad yourself." She looked at him without thinking of the audience anymore. "Are you going to give me any excuse for us going through this charade?"

Samuel shook his head. "The less you know, the safer you and your friends are." He pulled away from her and jumped out of the car, coming to the other side to help her out. Taking the package of food in one hand, he put his other on her back once again. They strolled to her house. It felt good. Sarah was feeling very guilty for having the feelings she was having.

He stopped at her door and leaned down. "I have to give you one more kiss. Are you ready?"

"No, you can't. Please. I can't do that to Jake again." She looked at his face. What she saw shocked her. It was obvious that he was in pain. What could make Samuel so afraid? She tried to make the tension between them lighter, "Oh, alright, but you have to promise it will be a short one."

Samuel smiled his real smile and pledged, "I promise to make this unbearable kiss a short one."

She smiled and without thinking she held his face and gave him a kiss instead of waiting for his. It wasn't as long as their first kiss, but the spark was still there. He wrapped his arms around her and pulled her close. She wasn't sure, but she thought she heard him moan. He pushed her back gently and said goodnight.

She turned and stepped inside the door. She turned around to find her mother staring at her. "What are you doing, Sarah? Be careful, my daughter. Don't forget where your loyalty lies. If you don't want Jake, that is fine, but just don't do it this way."

Sarah looked at her mother shocked. "What are you talking about, Mom? I want Jake so bad I can't breathe. This thing with Samuel isn't what you think it is. I promise." She searched her mother's face but saw disapproval instead of understanding.

"I see how flushed you are, Sarah. I know you're telling yourself you're just being friendly with the new neighbor, but it's getting to be too much very quickly . . . If you know what I mean." She looked at Sarah's lips.

Did she watch them from the window? Was she spying on them? She became angry with her mom. "I don't like it when you don't trust me. When did you feel you had to spy on me?" Sarah snapped. She didn't wait for an answer. She turned and rushed to her bedroom. Once she got in the door, she realized she still had the leftover food in her hands. She didn't care; she refused to face her mother again. She tossed the leftovers on the chest by her door and began getting ready for bed.

"Jake, come home quickly. I need you here." Sarah's words fell on silence. six more weeks until Jake would be home, and things would go back to normal. It had been only two weeks and look at the trouble she was in already. How had all of this happened? That stupid trail had caused all of this to happen to her. She had to tell Josh to stay away from the trail without telling him why he needed to stay away from the trail. Lovely. Now she felt like a spy or something.

That night didn't bring much sleep and the next morning Sarah was cranky. The bad thing about working for your mother is that when you have a fight the night before, you can't leave it at home. It goes with you to work the next day. Her mother tried to make conversation with her, but she felt violated, and if she were honest, she would have to say her mother was right. But she wasn't ready for that just yet. She hated being angry with her mom, but she also hated that her mom felt it was okay to spy on her.

Finally, her day of work was finished. Sarah was tired from the lack of sleep. She had stayed back in the records room all day thinking about what her mom had said last night. She hated to admit it, but her mom was right. She couldn't go on a date even a fake date with Samuel anymore. She would tell him just as soon as she saw him. She was sure he would pop up at some unexpected time. He always did.

That afternoon when she climbed into the van with her mom, she could hardly hold her eyes open. "I can't wait to get home and go to bed." Forgetting how angry she was, she looked at her watch; it was ten minutes after 4 o'clock. Oh no, she had forgotten to stop everything and think only of Jake. "Oh, Jake. I'm sorry. I wish you were here to help me with this predicament I have gotten myself into."

FOURTEEN

The following day, Sarah kept looking over her shoulder at the door in the waiting room. She expected to see Samuel walking in to make her life even more of a mess. Luckily, the day went by quickly and by noon Sarah was relaxed and playing with the animals in the waiting room.

Her mother came in from the field around 3 o'clock and came to the records room to find her daughter. She found Sarah filing and walked over to her and put her hand on the folder Sarah was getting ready to file. Sarah looked up at her mother, ashamed of her behavior. She was stressed, not wanting to explain her actions. Joyce would only worry, and Sarah didn't want to burden her mom with the craziness she was living through at the moment. "I'm sorry Mom," she offered.

Joyce nodded, "I'm sorry, too. Honey, you know that I'm your biggest supporter. I just don't want you to find yourself in a situation where you have cut ties that can't be fixed. Think before you act. Okay?"

Sarah looked at her mom; she wanted more than anything to have someone to talk to about this mess, but she couldn't risk putting her mom in danger. Samuel had said they had to keep everyone safe -- from what she wasn't sure.

She searched her mother's face only to find concern for her daughter. "I am not going to mess things up with Jake, Mom. We love each other. It would take a much bigger force than Samuel to break us up. Samuel is just a person that doesn't know anyone here, and he has a weird family that has moved next door to us." She smiled a reassuring smile and hugged her mom.

Joyce accepted her daughter's words and went into the waiting room to visit with her remaining patients. At 4 o'clock Sarah stopped working on the files and sat down and thought of Jake. "Please come home soon, Jake. Please understand that what I have done is to keep our friends and families safe." She tried to imagine his face and found it hard to see him. It hadn't even been three weeks, and she was having a hard time seeing his beautiful, handsome face. She made a mental note to bring a picture of Jake to the office. She had a few on her phone but she wanted to have a constant reminder for others of her love for him. She wanted evidence for her mother and Samuel when he popped up at the office.

The ride home was quiet and relaxed. The stress of last night's conflict forgotten. Joyce and Sarah discussed the animals her mother had seen during the day. Sarah asked her mom what diagnoses she had made for Chester, a beautiful black lab that had been brought into the clinic earlier in the day. Chester had pleading eyes, asking Sarah to make him feel good again.

Sarah hoped her mother could help him; he was so friendly and loving. Joyce was on the verge of answering her daughter when her mouth dropped open. In front of them, a large semi-truck turned up Buffalo Creek. The slowness of the truck and the moan of the motor as it labored up the road made it obvious that it hauled something heavy. Just when they were getting used to seeing this large truck on their small road, Sarah noticed in front of them a concrete truck and in front of that was another. All the way up the road Sarah could only see the trucks and equipment rolling past their home.

"What on earth, Mom?" She attempted to close her shocked mouth but didn't succeed. When she tore her eyes from the crowded road to her mother's face, she found her mom just as dumbfounded as she.

They finally made it to their driveway and parked; giving room to the remaining vehicles that had accumulated behind them. When they entered their house, Sarah's father was peeking out the curtain at the front window. The road was full of trucks and equipment. Her father looked at the two of them and exclaimed, "What on earth could be happening on that farm that all of these construction equipment vehicles are needed? I have been watching for the past hour, and they haven't let up yet. I wouldn't believe it if someone told me this was happening if I hadn't witnessed it myself."

His face was as dumbfounded as Sarah's and her mother's. Sarah giggled. Her dad's reaction to the newness of the Lazra's was setting in. Her dad couldn't hide his uneasiness, which was totally out of character for him. 'Chill and let others chill' was his motto.

"Sarah, did Samuel say anything about this?" He gestured with his hands toward the highway. That brought Sarah out of her giggling stage. She looked at her dad and shook her head a definite no.

Joyce looked at her daughter. She noticed how nervous Sarah got when Samuel's name was mentioned. What was making her nervous, causing her to act strangely when it came to this new boy? What was Samuel doing to make her so fidgety? Was Sarah liking this boy too much and feeling guilty about how much she liked him? Joyce knew Sarah loved Jake but she was young, and Jake was not around. She hoped Jake got home soon.

Joyce wanted to see firsthand exactly what Samuel meant to Sarah. "Sarah, we need to ask Samuel and his family to dinner this week, let's say Thursday evening. Do you want to ask Samuel or do I need to make a stop at the farm tomorrow to invite his family?"

She didn't miss the fear that briefly filled Sarah's face. "No, I can take care of it, Mom. I'll call Samuel tomorrow. Okay?" Her face was near panic underneath the fake cheer she was trying to present to her parents. Joyce decided not to press Sarah's emotions for the time being. She would make sure she knew what was happening before the week was over. She loved her daughter, and somebody's head would roll if they made Sarah this miserable. She looked over Sarah's head at her husband, already focused on the TV. He was such a smart man to be so oblivious to his surroundings, including his family. Men!

The next day Sarah tried to contact Samuel. She didn't have a phone number, but with the clinic's access to the phone company's local numbers, she was able to get a number for the Lazra's home residence. Unfortunately, no one answered, though she had called throughout the morning. She decided to wait until after lunch to try again. She had to contact Samuel before her mother made the mistake of going to the farm. If Samuel was telling any truth, she feared what would happen to her mom. She would come clean before she would allow her mom to set foot on that creepy farm.

Joyce made it back to the clinic and brought Subway sandwiches for Sarah and herself. "So, have you contacted Samuel? Are his parents and he going to join us on Thursday?" She studied Sarah.

"I've been calling all morning, but he isn't answering. I'll keep trying after lunch."

Joyce dismissed the subject. "That's okay; I can swing by their place on my way from Leigh's this afternoon. I'd like to meet Samuel's family, and this is a good excuse to visit.

Sarah shrieked, "No! I'll contact Samuel. Please, Mom, you have to let me ask him. Please! Promise me you will not go up to the farm." Joyce watched as her daughter fought to gain her composure. What had these people done to her daughter? She held her anger in, trying to find out what was happening without asking or being a nosy mama.

After studying Sarah's stressed face, she relented, "Okay, I'll wait." She released her frustration, "I thought it would be an easy solution to track them down. It'd give me an excuse to see what's happening up there. But, I promise to wait until you ask Samuel first."

She watched her daughter's face transform from total panic to calm at least on the surface. Joyce struggled to contain her suspicions and anger for whatever was making her daughter this stressed.

Sarah continued calling Samuel throughout the afternoon without an answer. She was on the verge of panic when Samuel walked into the waiting room of the clinic. Sarah was never as happy to see a person, as she was to see Samuel. He glided over to the counter and greeted the staff in his polite but formal manner.

Sarah was too eager to speak with him to wait until he requested to see her. She burst through the doors leading to the waiting room and dragged him to the filing room. "Where have you been? I have been trying to call you all day."

In the midst of her frustration, she had not realized that she had him by his shoulders shaking him. She came out of her trance once she heard Samuel snickering. She looked him in the eyes with her own squinted eyes to prove how angry she was at him. Sarah's aggressive display made him bellow out in laughter. She didn't know Samuel possessed the ability to laugh in this manner. His laughter brought her back to reality, and she dropped her hands from his shoulders. He grabbed her around the waist and gave her a peck on the cheek. "You're cute when you're angry." He immediately realized what he had done and stepped back from her and apologized. "I am sorry, Sarah. I didn't mean to overstep my place."

Sarah found it hard to breathe. "I understand, Samuel, but I like my life. I like my boyfriend. Please don't think I am willing to forsake Jake."

Samuel shook his head in refusal. "I don't want you to feel you are betraying Jake. I'm only trying to keep you and Jake and your families safe. I apologize for overstepping my boundaries before." He was back to his serious, formal self.

"Why were you so anxious to see me? Did I do something wrong or did you just miss me?" He had found his sense of humor once again.

"Ha-ha," Sarah faked a dry laugh. "You do have a sense of humor. Who would have guessed?" She felt anger flush her face. She didn't know how she got so involved in this mess but she wanted Samuel and all of this to leave. She wanted her life back.

Sarah remembered why she was desperate to see Samuel. She must protect her mom from the unseen danger that Samuel constantly warned her about. "Samuel, I need to invite you and your parents to come to dinner on Thursday. My mom has made it a mission to invite your family over for dinner, and she won't budge from the idea. Do you think you can talk them into coming?"

Samuel's face clouded over. "My parents will be out of town on Thursday. They will be gone all week this week and next week." He quickly added, "I would love to come for dinner if the invitation still stands."

Sarah's frustration was evident. She looked at Samuel with a frown and barked, "You will have to do. Mom will expect someone for dinner, so you have to come." Still frowning she told Samuel to be at her house at 6:30 on Thursday. And if perchance any of his relatives--who were safe-- could make dinner, it would be a blessing.

"If you knew my mom, you would know that she doesn't give up once she gets an idea in her mind. I am scared she will show up on your doorstep. Please don't allow anything to happen to my mom."

Samuel had been amused with Sarah's sharp commands of him until he heard what had gotten her so frustrated. "You're right to be concerned, Sarah. We must keep her away from the farm. If I can get my parents back to Salyersville, and if I can persuade my parents to come with me to dinner on Thursday, you and I must show affection toward each other. It will be expected." He dropped his eyes to the floor as if the white tile in the files room was the most important thing in his life. Once he gathered his nerves he declared, "we have to continue this charade."

Sarah frowned. "I cannot show affection toward you when my parents are there to witness it. That's impossible. You have to think of something else. I hate this, Samuel."

"I know I have put you in a horrible position. Maybe I can come over, and we can have a lover's quarrel. That way my family and the farm will realize our relationship was not meant to happen. What do you think? If we argue will your parents still insist on meeting my family?"

"I'm not sure that you and I are the reason my mom wants to meet your parents, but it's worth a try. I can even say that I wished she wouldn't push the dinner thing because you and I are on such bad terms." She smiled at Samuel.

"Good, then it's a deal. I'll come to dinner, and we will be friends in front of your parents, and then we will argue. What could we argue about that your parents will believe?" True to Samuel's personality, he didn't give away any emotions he was feeling about the arrangement. Sarah couldn't tell if he was sad that they would not be friends after this, or if he was relieved to be rid of his fake girlfriend.

"Let's just wait until the evening begins and see what opportunity arises," she said, almost to herself rather than to Samuel.

"Okay with me," Samuel agreed.

FIFTEEN

Sarah waited until her mom was cooking to break the news that only Samuel would be coming for dinner. "He sends his apologies. He thought his parents were coming back from New York today, but they're delayed." Sarah fumbled with the silverware pretending to be busy setting the table. She didn't satisfy her mother's questioning eyes.

Joyce looked at her daughter but couldn't catch her eyes. She suspected that Sarah was deliberately keeping her eyes averted from her. The question of why her daughter wasn't completely honest with her kept nagging at her. Why did she wait until dinner was being made to spring this on her? She knew from experience that pumping Sarah for more information was useless. Once her daughter closed up, no one could get her to share anything. Joyce had seen her too many times with this same look on her face. She decided to keep her thoughts to herself for the moment. She would have to be very observant during dinner.

Sarah was relieved when the doorbell rang. Finally, the beginning of the end for this crazy situation that was happening. She opened the door and found Samuel standing as handsome as ever in a yellow polo and khakis. He had a bouquet of spring flowers for her mom. He was thoughtful for someone completely absent of emotions. He looked above her head to check for her parents. When he was sure they were alone, he told her, "I have to give you a kiss, Sarah. Are you ready?" He came closer and motioned behind him with his eyes. As if saying, "They are watching." Sarah understood and leaned forward.

Samuel caressed the back of her head and looked into her eyes. If she hadn't known this was an act, she would have been knocked off her feet by his blue eyes. It was hard to remember that she had a boyfriend. She wanted to kiss Samuel, and she wasn't thinking about who was watching or about the boyfriend she hadn't seen in four weeks.

Samuel's lips caressed hers so very gently and then became firmer and demanding. His kiss for a show was taking her breath away. Sarah found herself meeting his demands with her own demands. Their goodbye kiss was a kiss that would not soon be forgotten. After only moments or maybe minutes, Samuel pulled away from her and looked down into her flushed face. His face constricted with emotion. What was the emotion she saw in his eyes, hurt, pain, and sadness? She couldn't be sure. She was too busy trying to control her runaway emotions. She couldn't put a label on them either.

Samuel cleared his throat and moved his hands from her face and neck to her shoulders. He turned her around and followed her into the house. He closed the door behind them. Sarah was embarrassed. What must he think of her if she couldn't kiss a strange boy without losing her wits? She straightened her shoulders, shook her head and called into the kitchen, "Mom, Samuel's here."

Joyce came rushing out to greet him. "Hello, Samuel. I'm glad you could come back to visit again. I'm sorry Dan and I couldn't be here during your last visit with Sarah. I do wish your parents had been in town so that we could have welcomed them to our little community." Joyce was well aware of Samuel and Sarah's flushed faces. She was trying very hard to act as if the scene in front of her was common. She was still interested in knowing the new neighbors, so she asked," Where are your parents this week?"

Sarah answered, "Mom, I told you Samuel's parents got delayed in New York, remember?"

Joyce smiled, "Oh yes, New York. Come in Samuel and have a seat. Dinner should be ready in about fifteen minutes. My husband should be home any moment. Sarah, you keep Samuel company while I finish up dinner." She turned and left the room without waiting for an answer.

Left alone again, Sarah and Samuel were feeling self-conscious from their earlier encounter. What was going on with them? Sarah refused to acknowledge what had happened at the front door while Samuel stared at her as if she had the answer to what had just happened.

Sarah lamely tried to make small talk. "So,

Samuel, what are you doing all summer? Now that you're stuck on Buffalo Creek, what do you do with all your time?" She searched for something to look at, anything except for Samuel's piercing eyes. Finally, her eyes came to land on Samuel.

He had regained his normally emotionless face. He cleared his throat before answering, "I've found living on the farm to be stimulating. The horseback riding is fascinating and working on getting the farm in proper order has taken most of my time. How about you, Sarah; what are you doing with all of your time since your boyfriend abandoned you for the summer?"

Sarah's eyes snapped with anger. "Jake hasn't abandoned me. He was lucky enough to get an invitation to study pre-med at the University of Kentucky this summer. It was a very sought after invitation and Jake was chosen from many vying for the chance. I'm very proud of him and also very happy for him." Take that Samuel Lazra, she thought.

Samuel did take that. He smirked, "Okay, but what are you doing during your spare time? I only heard about what Jake was doing this summer, nothing about your summer."

Sarah was seething when her dad entered the house. Samuel graciously stood and shook her father's hand. "I'm pleased to meet you, sir." Samuel offered.

Sarah's dad replied, "Well, I'm pleased that I finally get to meet our new neighbor. I wish your parents could have made dinner. I feel a little embarrassed that we haven't had them over to welcome them yet."

"They're very busy, sir. They don't get out into the neighborhood much." Samuel stated matter-of - factly. "Both of my parents are very active business people. They travel a lot of the time."

Dan quizzed more, "So what brought you guys to Buffalo Creek? Do you have relatives here? That's how most people find their way to our neck of the woods. It's not like we have anything to offer other than our friendly neighborhood."

Samuel didn't allow his frozen facial features to show any emotions. "No, I don't have any relatives here. I'm not sure how, but my father found out about the Gamble Farm and decided it was what our family needed. It's a good place to relax and get away from the rat race for a while. I love to ride, and the farm gives me plenty of room for my horses."

Dan pushed on, "You sound like you came from the city, Samuel. Where did you learn to ride?

Samuel smiled, "The school I attended for years has stables and my father housed my horses there so that I could have something to keep me busy during my idle time." It wasn't difficult to hear the bitterness in Samuel's voice.

Dan wasn't satisfied yet, "I've noticed all of the equipment and supplies that are making their way to your farm. You guys must be making a lot of changes to the property."

Sarah was aware that the smile that Samuel gave her father was his fake one. "We are indeed. My father is making a beautiful place from a desolate farm we bought only weeks ago."

Sarah's mom entered the room announcing dinner. They all made their way into the dining room while Sarah's mom took up where her father left off. Poor Samuel was getting the fifth degree of questioning. He held his composure very well. Sarah had to smile at her parents' tag teaming Samuel. They were determined to find out what was going on up the road before they released him.

Once dinner was over, Sarah felt sorry for Samuel. He had endured the fifth degree from her parents throughout the whole meal.

"Would you like to go down to the barn while I feed my animals? I'll introduce my horse, Heine, to you."

Sarah felt Samuel's look pierce into her very soul. He nodded without speaking and led the way to the door. Once out of the earshot of her parents, Samuel stopped Sarah midway to the barn. "Sarah, I will miss our fake relationship. I hope we can remain friends after all of this is finished."

Sarah linked her arm through Samuel's and pulled him toward the barns once again. She couldn't resist him if she wasn't busy doing something. Working in the barn would help her to think rationally. Once at the barn, she trusted herself to speak to Samuel. "You know I am your friend, Samuel. I think we both realize that we have a strong friendship after all that has happened to us this summer. I don't want to lose your friendship either. It is my deepest wish for you to become a part of our group of friends. I know everyone will become friends of yours just as I have. They just have to get to know you." She smiled up at Samuel. She wasn't sure, but she thought she saw a tear ready to spill.

She felt her own heart aching for what was happening with them tonight. Why? They were not real boyfriend and girlfriend. Why did it feel like they were breaking up for real? She reached her hand up to Samuel's face to wipe the tear away, but he caught her hand and kissed it. She searched his eyes questioning what was happening when he bent to her face and kissed her. It was a tender, loving, goodbye kiss. She knew in her heart that this wasn't part of the act. This was Samuel saying goodbye to her. She felt she was watching the scene from above as she kissed Samuel. She couldn't deny that she had feelings for him.

After a long embrace, they stepped away from each other while still holding hands. Sarah was the first to break the spell. She felt guilt for what she was doing with Samuel. What was she doing?

She desperately tried to remember Jake. Why did she find it hard to remember her darling Jake? Yet, here she was straining to turn this fake relationship with Samuel into the past, and she was genuinely sad. Guilt clouded her face as she tried to regain her composure.

She decided to go to the familiar. She glanced at Samuel and quietly asked, "Do you want to meet my horse, Heine?"

Samuel shook his head in refusal. His voice strained. "I think we should go back to the house and continue our discussion we were having before dinner." He looked at Sarah with his piercing eyes. "We can finish our talk about the infamous Jake and his abandonment for the summer." He watched her face flush with anger. His strategy was working. "How long has he been gone; leaving you with boys like me circling, just waiting to take his place?" He moved closer to her.

She stepped back away from him and demanded, "What do you think you are doing?" She shot fire back at him. "You have no right to be getting this familiar with me. I have tried to be kind to you, but this is ridiculous." She felt like hitting him. How dare he talk about Jake as if he had done something wrong just because he had gone away for the summer? People do these kinds of things all the time.

Then, it dawned on her; Samuel was making her angry so when they said goodbye it would look believable to those watching. Samuel watched as the truth seeped through Sarah's eyes. She smiled at him, and he smiled back. He took her still warm hand in his and led her back to the house. Once they were back in the living room, Samuel began his taunting again. "Why would Jake leave you here all summer long without even trying to see you, Sarah?"

She played along with his lead. "I think it's about time you went home, Samuel." Her eyes had lost their anger and now were filled with endearment. Samuel was a good person. Irritating for sure, but he was trying to do the right thing for her friends and family--and for her as well.

She stole a long look at him. He was her age but completely alone in a home that made him fear for those around him. It must be horrible to live in a house where you couldn't feel safe with your family around you. She wanted to pull him to her and cradle him. She wanted to tell him that things would be okay. She remembered her mission and so instead of hugging him, she raised her voice. "How dare you speak about Jake in that manner. This evening is over. Leave my home." She heard her father and mother rushing to the living room.

Her father stopped short when he saw them standing near the door. Joyce was going too fast and bumped into Dan before she could stop. She wedged past her husband; bounding into the room to fix whatever had gone horribly wrong. "What is going on here? We could hear your voices all the way in the kitchen." She looked first at Sarah and then at Samuel. Both faces were flushed, but it wasn't anger on either face she saw. Samuel was trying to pull off anger, but looked sad and longingly down at Sarah. Surprisingly, her daughter's face wasn't filled with anger either, although her voice would have made them believe she was furious. Sarah was looking at Samuel with a sadness Joyce had not seen her daughter possess before. It was obvious that Sarah had fallen for Samuel or at least felt a closeness toward him.

Samuel broke the spell and pulled his eyes away from Sarah. "I think I had better be going. Thank you for your hospitality and dinner. I enjoyed the evening until this incident." He turned his gaze back to Sarah. The look held regret and goodbye. He opened the door and motioned for her to follow. They had to show this enactment for the viewers outside.

Sarah stepped outside with him and began their conversation all over again. "How dare you talk about Jake as you have tonight. He is a wonderful person and doesn't deserve you putting him down, especially since he isn't here to defend himself."

Samuel used this as an opening, "I thought you had forgotten him, Sarah. I thought you and I had a chance for something, but I guess I was wrong." He looked at her eyes reflecting hurt--she was sure it was hurt.

Her eyes were filled with the same pain while her heart ached. Why was this happening? She only wanted to be faithful to Jake. True, Samuel made it hard for her to be loyal to the boyfriend she thought she could never be unfaithful to, but here she was, dying inside because she was losing this boy as a fake boyfriend. Did she feel sorry for him because he didn't have any friends in Salyersville or was it because she had become very fond of him? She remembered the kisses they had shared and admitted that there were sparks between the two of them.

"Leave, Samuel. We're finished here. Have a nice life." She didn't look into his face again. She couldn't bare it. She stepped back into the house and shut the door. She tried to keep anger on her face because she knew that her parents would be waiting. She just stood listening to the motor of the BMW start and then he was gone. She couldn't explain the sadness and loss she felt to anyone, especially to herself. She made herself look at her parents and just shrugged. She couldn't manage to say anything at the moment.

They seemed to understand. Her dad asked if she was okay. She shook her head yes and then made herself ask, "Is it okay if I go to my room for a while? I'm not feeling too well after all the arguing." Her parents both nodded a slow yes and watched as their daughter left the room and moved like an old woman up the stairs to her room.

The two looked at each other with their mouths

open. "What was that all about?" Dan asked. "I've never seen anything like that unless I watched it on a soap opera. It's not like Sarah to have such an angry argument with anyone, let alone a guest in our home." He looked at his wife in perplexed wonder.

Joyce, adrift in her puzzled thoughts, answered, "I don't know what is going on, but there is something strange about this whole situation. Sarah hasn't been acting like herself for several days now. At first, I thought it was because she was missing Jake, but I am beginning to suspect Samuel has something to do with the matter."

Dan, oblivious to his daughter's interest in Samuel, asked, "What do you mean when you say it has something to do with Samuel?'"

"Isn't it obvious? Sarah acts funny whenever we mention Samuel or his family. She gets skittish, and I don't know why. I was hoping that something would reveal itself during dinner, but I am just as in the dark as I was before dinner."

Dan looked at his wife. "How long have you been concocting this theory, Angela Lansbury?" He laughed at his joke. When Joyce didn't join in, he became serious again. He cleared his throat, "Sorry."

Joyce didn't allow Dan's humor to stop her; she was on a roll, and she wanted to see where it would end. "Do you remember when we all heard about the Gamble Farm? Sarah and her friends were sad because they had lost their playground. And then Sarah invites Samuel over to our house."

"Does that sound like our Sarah, only days after Jake leaves; she invites another boy to the house? And then, she takes him to Leigh's to play cards?"

"Everywhere she is, Samuel seems to show up. Why?" She stopped to take a breath. She looked at Dan as if for an answer.

"I agree. Sarah has been acting funny. I'm not sold on the romantic thing with Samuel and her, but she is acting weird about Samuel and his family. Did you notice how nervous she got when she thought we were going to have the Lazra's over for dinner? It didn't surprise me that only Samuel made it to dinner. Where are his parents? Does he have parents?"

Joyce looked at him just to make sure he was

serious, and she saw that indeed, he was serious. She thought about what he had said. "We have not seen anyone from Gamble Farm except Samuel. Everyone else in the family is keeping to themselves. Who doesn't get out in town to see what the place they just moved to has to offer?"

Joyce's face began to light up. "She got very anxious when she thought I was going over to the farm to invite Samuel's parents to the house in person. She was near panic. It was to the point that I backed off and allowed her to invite them through Samuel. I believe there is something about the Lazra family buying the Gamble Farm that's making Sarah act the way she's been acting this summer. I can't imagine what it could be but I will find out."

She reached for her husband's hand and led him into the living room where they sat on the couch, Dan rubbing his wife's feet while deep in thought. "Samuel seems to be the central object in this equation. Maybe he can give us some answers."

"That is what I thought when I invited him over tonight. But you saw how that turned out." Joyce waved toward the entryway as if Samuel and Sarah were still standing there arguing. "I just don't buy the loud arguing bit. They were staging the whole thing. Did you look at their faces? Anger was the last emotion I saw on either of their faces."

Dan was again shaking his head in agreement. "Which brings us back to why."

Joyce pulled her feet down to the floor off of her husband's lap and kissed his cheek. "I don't know why, but I intend to find out." She pulled Dan up from the couch and headed upstairs. "Let's go to bed and think about it some more tomorrow." Dan eagerly followed his wife.

SIXTEEN

Joyce was quiet and mindful of her daughter's anxious mood while the two rode to the clinic the next morning. Sarah was thankful that her mother was allowing her time to process what was going on with her today. Should her mother ask for an explanation for the incident that happened the night before, she wouldn't know how to explain her behavior. She glanced at Joyce, who was obviously struggling to keep her opinion of the evening before to herself. Sarah smiled as she watched her mother, maybe she wouldn't have to explain. Although, she'd never known her mom to leave things unsettled. She would just wait and try to be ready when Joyce decided to begin her interrogation.

Joyce was deep in thought, trying to decide what to do about Samuel and his family. She had to find out what was going on with her daughter. She hated to see Sarah so stressed over what--what could it be that was making her so stressed?

Joyce realized Sarah was missing Jake. That was a given. But this was more than a girl missing a boyfriend. She stole a glance at Sarah and saw the worry on her face.

"Are you feeling better this morning?" Joyce asked. She wanted to test the waters to see if Sarah was open to discussing what was going on with her.

Sarah braced herself for the impending interrogation. "I feel better. I don't know why I allowed Samuel to get me so angry last night. He was putting Jake down, and I lost my temper. I'm sorry Mom. I know better than to act in that manner." She hoped that was enough to satisfy Joyce.

Sarah's explanation and apology worked in keeping Joyce from going into complete interrogation mode. One look at Sarah and anyone could see that she was miserable and sorry about the previous night's argument. Her face was pale, and she chewed her lip while twisting a lock of her hair continuously. Joyce knew her daughter only did these things when she was nervous. She had chewed her lip and twisted her hair ever since she was a toddler when she was in trouble or upset about something.

Seeing Sarah revert to these nervous ticks was a sure sign that she was on edge. Joyce decided to leave her alone for the time being. Sarah needed time to rest from all that was going on with her and Samuel and with her and Jake. She wished Jake could call home or allowed visitors. If Sarah could see Jake, it might put things into perspective. Sarah was almost seventeen, but not nearly old enough to deal with the situations in which she had found herself. Joyce realized that whatever her daughter did or didn't do would affect the rest of her life. She had to help her without influencing her decisions.

The day went by faster than Sarah had anticipated. She finished her work in the file room and sat waiting for her mother to return from her rounds when she heard the phone ring in her mom's office. She decided to answer Joyce's private line just in case she could help. It wasn't like she was busy solving her own problems. She smirked at the conversation she was having with herself.

She picked up the receiver and heard her mom

telling her she would be late because of issues with one of the horses on Allen Farm. Sarah felt relief flood through her body. The thought of not having to ride home with her mom gave her a much-needed break from her mother's quizzical eyes. Not that she didn't enjoy being with her mother on their rides to and from work, most of the time it was her favorite time of the day. But with things the way they were at the moment, she welcomed the space. She told Joyce she would hitch a ride with Becky, the receptionist, and she would see her later at home.

Sarah made her way to the front office to ask Becky if she could get a ride home with her this evening when she saw Leigh standing at the reception desk. "Leigh, it's good to see you. What brings you to the clinic?"

Sarah could see that Leigh was noticeably stressed. "One of my horses is down, and I need your mother, but Becky tells me she is out with another horse. I'm scared about Mem. I think I could help her if I had someone to assist."

Sarah didn't think twice. "I'll go with you. I know I can help too. I've helped Mom on several occasions, and I'm certain I know what to do. With the two of us, we should be able to save the foal."

Leigh's mood changed. "Bless you, Sarah. Can you come now?"

"Sure, let me get my purse." As Sarah followed Leigh to her pickup, she realized that she felt the best she had felt all day. She dismissed her worries about Samuel and concentrated on her friends. "How is Cassie? Doesn't she get to come home this week?"

Leigh brightened, "Yes, and I can't wait. The house is lonely without her there. I haven't even had any visits from the lady in white this summer."

Sarah laughed at Leigh's reference to her resident ghost. "I can't wait to see Cassie either. We should have a party for her. I'll talk with some of the gang that might be getting back to town, and we can have a picnic in your back yard if that's okay?" Sarah asked.

Leigh was bubbling. "I'd love to have everyone over. I'll talk with Josh, too. I'm sure he can help with inviting all your friends. Could you ask Samuel to come?" Leigh didn't even hesitate before going on to the menu. Sarah struggled to get past Leigh's request that she ask Samuel to attend.

She didn't have to answer Leigh because they arrived at the barn just in time to start the hard task of working on the mare. Sarah forgot all of the troubles that had been swirling around in her head and focused on saving the mare and foal.

She and Leigh made a great team. They worked until dusk. Once the foal was born, and Leigh felt like she could take care of the mother and new baby she asked, "Sarah, would you mind riding one of the horse's home? You can take Cassie's. I don't want to leave this little one alone just yet. I want to keep an eye on him and his mama for a while." She hugged Sarah. "Thank you so much for coming to our rescue. You're going to be an excellent vet one day, Sarah." Leigh turned her attention back to the mare. "Call me when you get home."

Sarah couldn't give any reason she shouldn't ride home over the hill except she had to pass by the Lazra's farm. Sarah remembered all too well Samuel's warning about coming too close to the farm. She tried not to think of what could happen. It was Buffalo

Creek after all. She'd lived here all her life. She got Cassie's horse ready and climbed on. She told Leigh goodbye and headed up the hill to the ridge. She hurried the horse trying to get past the dreaded Lazra's.

She didn't know if it was her mind or if she was hearing the familiar sound of something following her. Was Samuel following her again? She didn't want to talk to him yet. She was still trying to forget their kiss at the dinner date last night. She sped up, and the hooves behind her sped up also. The faster she nudged her horse, the faster the hooves behind her sounded. They were getting louder and closer. Her horse was getting skittish and began balking when she insisted he go faster. She made it to the end of the ridge and slowed so she could make it down the hill to her farm. Just as she released a breath of relief, she was knocked off the back of her horse.

She felt her breath leave her and in slow motion saw the dirt come toward her face. She felt pain rack her body. She was vaguely aware of being smothered by something or someone. It wasn't Samuel. Samuel would never hurt her like this. She couldn't see what was attacking, but got glimpses of dark moisture covering her. It was like a mist that was enveloping her in a freezing agonizing cold.

It was heavy and kept making her struggle just to keep conscious. She rolled trying to make it to her horse that had stopped at the edge of the clearing before beginning the decline down the hill. She felt the rocks and twigs from the pasture eating into her skin as she dragged her body, desperately trying to make it to her horse. Before she could get to her horse, she felt something yanking and pulling her lower half; almost as if it was consuming her inch by inch, making its way to her head.

Just as she felt life leaving her, she sensed the cold lifting from her body. Finally, she was breathing easier. She began struggling toward the horse once again. As she struggled, she felt arms pick her up and carry her. She wanted to fight but didn't have the energy to move, let alone fight for her safety. Then she lost consciousness.

SEVENTEEN

When Sarah opened her eyes, she was resting in a soft bed. Her body was so weak that she couldn't move her head to see where she was. All she could see from where she lay was that the room was gray with white curtains covering large windows. She realized that she had never seen this place before. Where was she? Did she die? She couldn't distinguish if she was too scared to find out or didn't have the energy to care. She saw the outline of a person coming toward her; then there was nothing.

When Sarah became alert once again, she saw the same scene she remembered from the first time she awoke. She tried to search for a person or at least something familiar. She felt something cold on her forehead. Was someone trying to help her? She didn't know. If she could see a face, she might know if it was friend or foe. She tried to move her head so she could see the face but she lost consciousness again.

She woke again. This time, the white curtains were pulled back, and she could see the outside landscape. It looked familiar, but she couldn't determine where she was. She wondered if her parents missed her yet. No doubt they would be worried. She wished she could tell them she was alive, but she wasn't able to make her body move. This time, her alertness lasted longer. She could tell because she watched the sun move across the porch outside the window. Hopefully, this meant she was beginning to stay awake for hours instead of minutes.

Where was the person who had been there before? Was she left alone to die? She thought someone was trying to help her. She remembered a cold cloth being pressed to her forehead.

She slept, but this time, it was different. Before she had lost consciousness, this time it felt like naps that she had taken during days when she was home from school because of the flu. She woke with a start. She wondered if she was having a nightmare, but when she focused her eyes, she was still in the gray room. She looked at the window and saw the dark of night showing from outside. She was positive that her parents would be searching for her.

Cassie's horse surely made it back to Leigh's. Leigh would have contacted her parents. Would they be able to find her? Where was she?

When Sarah woke again, she could see daylight through the window. She moved her arms and felt a sense of healing throughout her body. She felt stronger than the last time she was awake. She moved her head and her upper body around in the bed to get a better look at her surroundings. The room was well decorated, and she guessed that someone liked antiques. Sarah could tell that the furniture was of the best quality, and she would guess that it belonged to a man. The room was nice but didn't have the frills that most women enjoyed. From what Sarah was seeing, the owner of the room wasn't evident. She scanned the room for something that would tell her where she was but found no pictures or other things to give her clues.

She wondered when the person would come back to her. She didn't know how long she'd been in this room, but she was anxious to be out and back to her room, her home, and her life.

As she began drifting back to sleep, she heard the sound of footsteps coming toward the room. Her heart began to quicken. What if this person wasn't trying to help her? Who were they? She would find out soon. The door began to open, and she held her breath. She was still weak and in no condition to defend herself. As the door opened, she saw a familiar face. Samuel stood in front of her bed. But he was old. It was like seeing Samuel thirty years in the future.

He moved toward her and began examining the gashes that striped her arms. She couldn't see the rest of her body, but if the pain was any indication, she was covered with cuts and gashes. She wasn't sure, but Samuel sounded as if he was crying. Was he crying because of what he had done to her? If he didn't do this, then how had he found her? Should she be afraid of him?

"Samuel, what happened to me?" Her voice sounded like someone else far away. She searched his face for an answer. "Do my parents know where I am? They must be worried."

Samuel's face filled with pain. She wanted him to say something-- anything that would give her a sense of familiarity. But, he didn't speak. He didn't attempt to speak. He didn't or wouldn't acknowledge that she had spoken to him. He searched her face for something; she wasn't sure what he wanted from her. She tried to speak again but was so weak that she couldn't. She began to feel herself losing consciousness again.

When she woke, the room was empty. She felt that she was gaining more strength and could move around in the bed with more ease. She wanted to get out of bed but knew her legs wouldn't hold her up, so she laid waiting for Samuel's return.

She thought about his visit. Samuel wasn't himself. He was wrinkled and stooped. He hadn't acted the same as the Samuel she had gotten to know this summer. He would never leave her without explaining what had happened to her. What was going on with him and why had he brought her to this place? She had been close to her farm when she'd been attacked. Why hadn't he taken her home instead of here?

Samuel had been silent when Sarah asked these questions of him; he hadn't answered her questions about her parents or about what happened to her. Was Samuel her friend or was he proving to be dangerous? She didn't want to think that the Samuel she knew would hurt her. But, here she was, and she hadn't seen what had attacked her in the woods. She had to regain her strength so she could escape.

She wasn't sure where she was, but she thought or hoped that she was on the Gamble Farm. The farm had changed so much lately that she couldn't be sure she would recognize it from what she remembered.

She'd heard or dreamed of equipment and hammering noises close to the room where she lay. She remembered the equipment that had passed her farm going toward the Gamble Farm. And then there was Samuel. Even though he hadn't taken her to her home, he would surely take her somewhere close; maybe to his home. She felt tired and could feel herself slipping into oblivion again.

The next thing Sarah knew she was sitting up in bed while an older man – not Samuel -- rummaged through a black bag that rested on a chair that sat next to the window she had been looking out to determine where she was. He was a tall, skinny man with a full head of gray hair that spilled over his head. His wire-rimmed glasses sat low on his nose, and he pulled his head back to look through them when he noticed her moving in bed. He faltered as he labored closer to the bed and peered down close to her face, looking at her eyes.

Sarah began asking the same questions of this man that she had asked Samuel. She stared at the strange old man, "Who are you? Where is Samuel? Where am I? What happened to me?"

She waited for answers as the old man busied himself with his bag. He didn't respond. The room fell silent. Sarah could feel her heart start to pound. What was wrong with these people? Why was everyone silent? First Samuel, and now this old man was silent.

Without looking in Sarah's direction or giving her any indication that he was leaving, the man turned away. He seemed to float out of the room. As much as Sarah had wanted someone to help her, she was glad this eerie person had left. She felt relieved to be alone in the room again. She tried moving and realized she was stronger than she had been before. If only she could push herself to sit up, her strength would return with the flow of her blood. She pushed with her elbows and tried not to scream from the pain of her scratches, as they pulled open from the strain. She couldn't help but whimper as she made herself raise her head from the pillow and pulled with her inner core to sit up in the bed.

Finally, she was able to sit on the bed. She held her breath, trying to remain focused instead of screaming out in pain. If she screamed, she wasn't sure who or what would visit her. Would it be friend or enemy? She couldn't take a chance in this place. Things were too weird here. She had to escape and she would, as soon as she could stand. At that moment she felt her body giving away to the black of unconsciousness once again. She sank back into the pillow; her efforts of sitting lost for the moment.

Sarah opened her eyes to sunshine streaming through the window. It was daytime, and she felt a surge of energy. She attempted to raise her head from the pillow and without much effort sat up in the bed. If it was this easy to sit up, maybe she could sit on the side of the bed. She threw her legs one at a time over the edge of the bed and raised her body. She maneuvered her way to the side, feeling her head giving into dizziness. She willed herself to stop and focus.

She waited and after a few moments, her will won. She was able to sit on the side of the bed and look around the room with more alertness than she'd had since the attack.

She still couldn't detect anything that would help her determine where she was or how to get help. She felt anxious and full of despair because she was stuck here in this room while her life was a void in the real world. She thought of her parents and what they must be feeling after days of her missing. What would she say once she got back to civilization? Would anyone understand what she had been through or believe her when she told of her ordeal?

As she stared at the sun shining through the window, she saw a shadow pass by the opening of the window. Sarah felt her heart begin to pound in her chest. What or upon a closer look, who was passing by her room? She tried to see the person, but all she could get a glimpse of was the back of a man's head. He was tall, and his hair looked dark. He moved slowly past the house without losing stride, almost as if he was wearing roller skates.

The sun kept Sarah from seeing closely, but she felt like this person could be Samuel. Sarah reasoned from the structure of his head and his height that the individual had to be Samuel. But surely, if Samuel were this close to her, he would help her. She decided to call out to the person and risk the danger of it not being Samuel.

"Samuel. Come back. I need you to help me. Help, Samuel!" she screamed.

She sat on her bed, resigned to the fact that whoever was outside the window didn't acknowledge that she was making any noise at all. The person kept moving without acknowledging what was happening on the other side of the window. "Samuel, don't leave me, please." Sarah pleaded. Why wasn't he stopping? Surely he could hear her pleading for help. But the figure moved on without stopping. It was as if the windowpane kept her voice silent. She screamed and shouted, crying as the person passed the window leaving only the sun streaming through. She felt weak and defeated. Would she never get out of this place?

Why was she being kept here?

She forced herself to her feet; waiting until she felt steady. She moved slowly away from the bed, one step at a time. She felt joy begin to rise inside as she slowly moved toward the door of the room. When she made it to the door and reached to turn the doorknob; her joy fell at her feet. The door wouldn't budge. She was locked in this place. She couldn't believe this was happening.

Maybe the window would offer a way out. She turned, panic-stricken and began the long journey across the room to the window. She felt the energy drain out of her body, and she decided to rest before attempting to climb out the window. She had no idea what lay in wait once she found a way out. She would need a lot of energy to make her way home. Once on the bed, she felt her body press heavily onto the bedding. She fell asleep.

The next time Sarah woke she heard the voice of someone calling her name. "Sarah. Sarah. Are you okay?" She opened her eyes to see Samuel in front of her. His face filled with fear and concern. She tried to rouse herself to comprehend what he was saying.

She struggled to sit up in bed while Samuel gently pulled her up into a sitting position. "Sarah, we must get you out of here. It's not safe within the confines of this farm."

She looked at Samuel. "Where are we? What farm is this, Samuel? Do you know what happened to me?" She struggled to ask, "Why didn't you talk to me, Samuel?" She wanted to know so much more but didn't have the energy to ask. Instead, she allowed Samuel to put her arm around his neck as he pulled her up and off the bed. He half dragged her, half carried her out of the room. Sarah's mind wondered how he had opened the locked door she had attempted to open only a short while ago. At least she felt like it was only a while ago when she had tried but failed to escape. She didn't have long to wonder; Samuel was helping her out of the gray room -- the room she was beginning to believe she would never leave.

Once out of the room, Samuel picked Sarah up and swiftly carried her out of the house. He loaded her onto a four-wheeler that was waiting for them and climbed onto the front, pulling Sarah's arms around his waist. She held on with what little strength she had and rested her head against his back. She felt his muscles tighten as they began moving up the road toward a tall rock wall. In the middle of the wall was an open gate.

Samuel drove through the gate stopping just outside. He jumped off the four-wheeler and ran over to the massive, solid gate, pushing until it snapped shut. Once he had the gate secured, he ran back to Sarah and took his position on the four-wheeler. This time, when they began moving, he went faster than before. Sarah thought his speed meant a fast get away. She tried to look from behind the shield of Samuel's back to see if she recognized any of the landscape. She had never seen the rock fence before, but the rest of the landscape looked familiar to her. Was she on the ridge that separated Samuel's and her farms? She felt her heart pound. Could she be going home?

Samuel slowed the four-wheeler at the bottom of the hill and pulled near the fence railing, following it all the way down to the Arnett's barns. Sarah was never as excited or relieved as she was the moment she saw the familiar barns and her horse in the pasture. She breathed a deep breath and whispered in Samuel's ear,

"Please hurry, Samuel, I need to see my parents."

Samuel pumped the gas, and the four-wheeler picked up speed. They moved across the pasture and over the road into Sarah's driveway. She jumped off the four-wheeler without waiting for Samuel's help. She still felt weak, but the surge of energy she had from the anticipation of seeing her parents was enough to get her to the front door. She made it to the porch and her parents. Before she could speak, she felt her surge of energy leaving. Just as Samuel leaped to her side, she sank into his waiting arms.

EIGHTEEN

Sarah wondered if she was dreaming. She opened her eyes to see her parents looking down on her. Samuel was on her other side looking as anxious as her parents. Did the past days happen or were they only a bad dream?

She raised her arm to check out the scratches and yes, the pain and open wounds were still there. She did not have a bad nightmare; she had actually lived a bad nightmare. She tried to smile at her parents and Samuel, and all three let out sighs as if they had been holding their breath.

"My beautiful girl, you are safe at home," her mother whispered. Sarah had a hard time focusing but knew the tears were flowing because she felt them burn as they dripped on her arm. She couldn't determine if they were her tears or her mother's-- maybe both. Joyce squeezed Sarah's hand and held on as if holding her hand would send healing throughout her body.

After a few moments, Sarah's father leaned over mother and daughter and gave both a gentle hug. "I've called Dr. Williams. He's on his way, Sarah. Dr. Williams had been Sarah's doctor since she was a child.

Sarah's mother was busy checking her daughter's injuries. "Dr. Williams will check you out at home and then we'll decide if you need to go the hospital. I hope you're well enough for me to take care of you here. I've checked you, and as far as I can tell, you have shallow gashes on your limbs and trunk. Your head and, thank God, your face appears untouched."

Sarah only nodded. She looked at Samuel. "What happened to me, Samuel?" She looked deep into his eyes for answers not spoken. She couldn't tell if Samuel was just really good at hiding his emotions or if he had no idea of what had happened.

He shook his head. "I don't know, Sarah. Your parents called me Thursday evening when you didn't make it home from Leigh's. We began searching for you that night. I finally came home to change clothes, and when I did, you were in my house resting in the downstairs bedroom." His piercing eyes questioned Sarah. "Can you remember, Sarah? How did you get there?" He looked just as puzzled as her parents.

Sarah remembered the previous days. She knew she saw Samuel or someone that looked like Samuel at least twice before he spoke to her and helped her escape. Was it Samuel or someone else? She wanted to question him longer but at that moment, Dr. Williams rang the doorbell. After her doctor had checked her out, he agreed she would heal just as well at home as in the hospital, if not better.

Joyce was one happy mom. She wanted to keep her daughter close. She had been so scared for Sarah. Her mind had wandered to scary places. Every hour that had passed left her in a deeper panic than the hour before. When everyone decided to go home and eat and rest for an hour then meet to begin the search again, she felt defeated. She was near her breaking point when Samuel brought Sarah home. She would never forget him for this gift, but she had to wonder how Sarah had ended up at Samuel's home. She knew that Samuel had been with the search party the entire three days that Sarah was missing so he couldn't have been keeping her captive.

So, how did Sarah end up at his home and not remember how she got there? Surely the person responsible for Sarah's attack was someone connected with Samuel. Maybe one of his relatives that no one had seen?

Joyce forced herself to shelve her questions. Sarah needed to feel comfortable and safe. She had been through a hideous ordeal, but Dr. Williams had determined that Sarah's injuries stopped with the bruises and slashes.

Joyce thanked God for this diagnoses. She decided to shelve her questions for the time being and concentrate on taking care of her daughter. She would make herself wait to determine what happened three evenings ago on that ridge between Leigh's farm, Samuel's farm, and their farm. Something happened, and her daughter was proof.

She helped Sarah upstairs into her bed, tucked her in, and kissed her good night. She sat at her bedside until she was sure Sarah was asleep. She left the room; leaving the door open as Sarah had requested. She went downstairs to find her husband with a stiff drink in his hand. The drink was the only way she could visually detect her husband's state of mind. On the outside, he seemed his usual calm, caring self, except he never drank anything other than a little wine during dinner and that was only sometimes.

She slowly walked to him and held him close. "She is home, thank God, she is home." He said nothing but caressed Joyce's back while burying his head in her neck.

Finally managing to speak, he announced, "I contacted the sheriff and told him that Sarah is home, but she isn't sure of what happened on the ridge. I explained the attack and the cuts and bruises to him." He released his breath and struggled to keep calm. "They are going to check out the ridge tomorrow. I told him that Samuel found her at his house when he went to change clothes and rest. Sheriff said he would make a visit to the farm in the morning.

I told the sheriff that Samuel had been with us the entire time and couldn't have anything to do with her kidnapping. I thought it best that we deal with him ourselves." He turned toward his wife, "Joyce, he was with us the whole time. How could he be involved in this?" He looked at his wife wanting answers, then demanded, "You saw him when he brought her home. Wasn't he as relieved as we were?" He shook his head, "I just can't believe he was part of this thing."

Joyce turned to her husband, "I think you did the right thing. It will just get Samuel in trouble if he's innocent. He brought Sarah back to us. We have to talk with him later to make a judgment call on his participation."

They stood clinging to each other. Holding on for dear life; each trying to understand what had happened the past three days. Neither had a logical answer to any of the occurrences.

The next morning, Sarah woke with a start. For an instant, she was still in the gray room waiting for someone to help her. Then she remembered Samuel. He had come to rescue her. He had saved her. She was sure that she would still be in that room had it not been for Samuel coming to help her.

Who had put her in that place and why was she held in the room under a locked door? She would be finding answers. Were the people that Samuel warned her about the ones that had kidnapped her? He had warned her to stay away, and she hadn't listened. She remembered Samuel's face and his urgency when he demanded she stay away from his farm.

She rose up in bed and felt even more energy than the day before. She swung her legs over the side and pushed her body around to a sitting position on the side of her bed. She felt confident that she could make it to the bathroom by herself. It felt good to be able to go to the bathroom, and she wanted to clean her body.

She began her bath water. She heard her mother coming into the room. Concern plastered all over her face she asked, "Sarah, are you awake? What are you doing?"

Seeing her daughter running her bath water she winced. "Oh, Sarah, I'll get a bath ready for you. Dr. Williams left some meds for you to soak in for the cuts on your arms and legs. It'll pull the soreness from them and help keep an infection from occurring." Joyce was putting the powder in the bath as she spoke. "Do you need me to help you get in the tub?"

Sarah smiled at her mom. She shook her head, "I think I got this, Mom. You can leave the door open so you can hear. I want to soak and relax for a while if that's okay?"

Joyce shook her head and hugged her daughter. "Of course, you can soak for as long as you want just don't shrivel up!" They both laughed.

Sarah tried not to think of what she had been through. She wanted just to sit in the tub and think of Jake. Their time together seemed to be a lifetime ago. She missed him and their lives so much. Why had all of this happened to her? Would she be in this predicament if Jake had been around? She answered herself. She did think it would have been the same maybe worse because Jake would not have backed away from the trail. Worse things could have occurred to him and the others.

She was glad Jake and many of their friends had been away this summer. She fell asleep in the tub and woke startled. How long had she slept, she wasn't certain? She called to her mom. "Mom, I'm getting out. Do you think you could get me some soft PJs to wear?"

Joyce called from her room; "I already put them on your bed. Do you need me to help you?"

"No, I've got it," she shouted as she climbed out of the tub and into the large white terry cloth towel her mom had put out for her. She slowly made her way back to her bedroom and put on fresh PJs. She was tired, so she willingly climbed back into bed for yet another nap.

Later that day, Sarah heard her mom calling her name. She answered and sat up in bed. Wondering why her mom was calling instead of coming to her room. Joyce had been hovering near Sarah's bedroom all day. Not that Sarah minded. She felt the closeness of her mom comforting. She knew Joyce was fighting her urge to question her about the incident. She stayed the caring mother, not the questioning and getting to the bottom of this mother. Sarah appreciated her mother's effort to allow her time and space that she desperately needed.

While she was lounging around in her bed, she

noticed Cassie and Leigh standing in her doorway. She was extremely glad to see her good friend. She felt strength flow into her body as she squealed, "Cassie, you made it back. I am so happy that you've made it home. I've missed my friend." She reached her arms out for a hug and quickly pulled them back. She saw Cassie and Leigh's faces when they saw the gashes on her arms.

Cassie rushed to Sarah's bed and flung herself into her friend's arms. "I am so glad to be home. I've missed you, too. But Sarah, you didn't have to go to all this trouble just to get me to come home. I was on my way already." They both giggled.

Leigh interrupted the two. "Hey, you two, I want my hug. Sarah, I'm sorry I didn't bring you home that evening. I had no idea that there was danger lurking in our hills. I would never have allowed you to ride in the hills had I known what could happen."

Cassie snuggled in bed next to Sarah, "What exactly happened, Sarah? You have to tell us what happened in the woods." Cassie looked at Sarah and without flinching, "You have to tell us what you remember."

Sarah shrugged, "I don't remember large chunks of it."

Leigh, and now Joyce, was sitting on the edge of Sarah's bed. Cassie didn't give up. "Tell us what you remember, okay?"

Sarah nodded her head. "I was riding your horse home from your farm, and I had almost made it to the hill going down to our barns when something spooked the horse. He threw me. I tried to get back to him, but I couldn't make it. Something flung itself on top of me, and I couldn't breathe or fight back. I tried to pull away from it. I'd get away long enough to get a breath of air, and it would consume me again. I thought I was going to die. Then, it was like something pulled it off me, and I could breathe. It didn't attack me anymore. I felt someone … I think it was a young man or at least his arms felt young and muscular … pick me up and I don't remember anything else.

"The next thing I remember; I was waking up in a gray bedroom. It was full of beautiful antiques. There was a window, and that is how I sort of kept track if it was day or night."

She paused, allowing herself a moment to get control over the story she was reporting to her friends and her mother. "I thought I saw someone that looked like Samuel, but older. Then I saw an old man who I have never seen before. Neither spoke to me or tried to help me."

She shook her head as if trying to free her memories, "Maybe I was dreaming, I'm not sure what was real or a dream. When I began to get some of my strength back, I made it to the door. I tried to leave, but it was locked. I was too weak to work at getting free, so I decided to wait until I gained more of my strength."

"While I rested, Samuel found me and then he rescued me. The rest you know. We rode his four-wheeler to my house where we found Mom and Dad. The next thing I remember, I was lying on the porch floor with Mom and Dad and Samuel all staring down at me."

Joyce sat with her mouth open. "Honey, I am so glad it's over. We have to find this older man. He could be dangerous to the people in our community. From what you've said, he doesn't sound like a local person." Joyce turned to Leigh, "Can you think of anyone that would fit his description, Leigh?

Leigh seemed to be deep in thought, "I can't think of anyone around here that fits that description. And, there isn't anyone local that would do this horrible thing to any of us. Whoever is guilty of doing this horrible crime has to be someone that was passing through the community. I wonder if the people that Samuel's folks have hired might be to blame. I mean, he did take Sarah to Samuel's farm."

Joyce also nodded deep in thought. She had thought the same thoughts as Leigh. If Samuel wasn't involved, then it would stand to reason that someone familiar with the farm was responsible for this. This explanation would answer a lot of questions. She wanted to give Samuel the benefit of the doubt since Sarah trusted him. But she wanted answers, and she would get them.

As far as she was concerned, Samuel had a lot to explain. She made a mental note to speak with Samuel about the employees of the farm. She didn't want to disturb Sarah with these details. She glanced at her daughter and saw the white shade she had become. "Now you two have a good visit while Leigh and I have our visit." She motioned for Leigh to come with her, and the older women left the two teens to visit and catch up on what the summer had brought them.

Joyce digested what Sarah had told her. She took deep breaths and exhaled slowly. Leigh hugged her friend, and they walked downstairs to Joyce's office. Joyce was determined to record what her daughter had told her about the incident. She needed to get the details down in writing so she could study it for clues later. Leigh helped her get the details on the computer while she waited until Cassie finished visiting with Sarah.

Cassie snuggled close to Sarah. "Are you okay? You look like you have been through it, my friend."

A faint smile flitted across Sarah's face as she replied, "I'm just glad it's over. I have never been in any situation as horrifying as those three days."

Cassie asked again, "What happened, Sarah-- and don't leave out any details. Our moms aren't here now. What has been going on with you since I've been in Louisville? Mom said you brought Samuel over to play cards one night. What was that all about? What's going on, Sarah?" Finally, she finished and waited for Sarah's answer.

Sarah looked dumbfounded, "I truly don't know … everything and nothing. I'm going to start from the beginning. You stop me if you can figure out what happened. Please!" She took a deep breath which caught with frayed nerves as she retold her story.

"I guess it all started when we found out that Samuel's family had bought the Gamble Farm. I met Samuel in the parking lot at school, but it was only a moment of introductions. Then, we all rode our four-wheelers around the ridge by Samuel's farm and saw those men standing guard at the borders of the farm. After that, we stayed away from Gamble Farm except for a few times when we felt brave. Jake and you left for the summer, and I began working with my mom. Things were calm and not exciting; you know how Salyersville can be during the summer."

Cassie waited, expecting more from Sarah. When Sarah didn't volunteer any more information she asked, "How did you get with Samuel? When I left, we had only seen him a few times, and he was cold and distant. Now the two of you are best friends?"

Sarah glanced at Cassie. She didn't want her friend to get the wrong idea about Samuel and their relationship. "Samuel and I met up a few times. He was alone and wanted to meet some of the people here. My mom and dad wanted to invite his family over for dinner so that we could get to know them. When I asked Samuel to invite his family, he said they were away on business, but he could come. So, he did.

Then, I asked Leigh if we could have a card game so he could meet some of the neighbors. She agreed, and he met Josh, Mark, and Leigh that night. He has been close to the farm most of the summer and every time I am on the trail, he seems to pop up."

Cassie was alert to the change in Sarah's mood when she began talking about the new neighbor. She wasn't sure what was going on, but Sarah wasn't telling everything. She thought she saw fear in Sarah's manner. She didn't know what to ask to draw out the information that would help her friend. She tried once again, "Sarah, what kind of relationship has developed between Samuel and you?"

Sarah's face turned white and then pink. "Not the kind you are trying to insinuate!" She snapped. "We're friends, I guess. I can't put a definition on it. We're friendly, yet I don't know a whole lot about him. All I know is that he and his family are very secretive. I haven't heard of anyone in town that has seen any of the Lazra's except for Samuel."

Cassie's face was full of thought. She was obviously trying to absorb all that Sarah had told her. "No one in town has seen Samuel's parents? It has been a couple of months since they moved to Gamble Farm. How can they have been that secluded? They have to come out of there for supplies."

Sarah quickly declared, "No, Cassie, no one has seen his parents. And when anyone asks about them Samuel changes the subject or shuts down completely. From the small amount he has said about them, I think they must work a lot in New York. I feel sorry for him; he seems to be all alone."

Sarah perked up. She sat up in bed and looked at Cassie as if what she had to say must be expressed with facial expressions for understanding. "You would not believe the Gamble Farm, Cassie. They have built a six or seven-foot high rock fence that surrounds the entire perimeter of the farm. It looks like a fortress up there. I don't know what's going on. All I know is that whatever it is, it's something that makes Samuel think it's dangerous for us to be around."

Cassie looked down at her friend's slashed arms, "Apparently, he's right." The room became silent as both girls shrank into their thoughts. Cassie was the first to pull herself out of her thoughts to speak. "Okay, my friend, I have kept you away from resting and healing long enough today. I'm going to bid you goodbye until tomorrow." She made an exaggerated bow from the side of the bed and turned on her heels, not waiting for Sarah's objections. Sarah giggled and allowed her friend to leave without trying to persuade her to stay.

Once downstairs, Cassie faced her mom and Sarah's mom who pumped her for information. She gladly shared what she knew, but felt guilty when Sarah's mom's face dropped from disappointment when she wasn't able to give her any more information.

Joyce pleaded for her to visit again tomorrow

and Cassie assured her that wild horses couldn't keep her away. Sarah was her best friend. She had been loyal from the moment they'd met. She had missed her while spending time with her old friends in Louisville. She still liked hanging out with them but felt a closer connection with the gang that had become her friends while living in Salyersville.

After Cassie's visit, Sarah drifted off to sleep for the afternoon. When she woke for a moment, she thought she was still in the gray bedroom back on Gamble Farm. She began to struggle to get out of bed, which woke her up, and she realized she was safe in her bedroom and her bed. She called out to her mom, "Mom, are you close?" She heard her mother walking quickly up the stairs to her room.

"Hey, sleepy head. You've been sleeping for a while. How are you feeling this afternoon? Do you think you can eat some dinner tonight? We have your favorite, spaghetti."

Sarah was glad to see her mom and happy for a routine. "I'd love to have dinner with Dad and you. Shall we go down now?" She rose off the bed and began combing her hair.

Joyce watched her daughter and decided she would not protest her efforts to come downstairs and have dinner. She wanted things to get back to normal with her daughter. She also wanted her to gain her strength back so that she could find out what was happening with Samuel. She had talked with Samuel earlier in the day, and he seemed full of concern for Sarah. He wanted to visit, but Joyce asked that he wait until tomorrow. She wanted Sarah strong enough to deal with what had happened, and Samuel was a part of what happened, she just wasn't sure as to what extent.

Dinner proved to be relaxing for them all. Sarah's father made the time light by making her mother and her laugh throughout the meal. After dinner, they all curled up on the couch and watched TV shows beginning with "How I Met Your Mother" followed by "The Big Bang Theory."

Sarah knew her father was watching these shows just because he was aware that they were her favorites. If it had been any other time, he would have squirmed through maybe a third of them, then escaped into his bedroom to watch sports. She was so lucky to be loved so much by such great parents. She reached over and gave both fat sloppy kisses. They hugged her and acted as if kisses like these happened every day.

NINETEEN

The events of the next day mimicked the day before except Sarah was feeling much stronger. She felt almost like her old self. She felt well enough to suggest her mother go back to work. She knew how much the clinic depended on her mother. Unfortunately, it was impossible to tell animals the best times to get sick. Her mom refused the suggestion but said if Sarah felt as well tomorrow then she would go in for a few hours.

Sarah lounged around the house watching TV, lying in the sun by the pool, sitting in the sunroom with her mother while they both read from their large selection of magazines. Life was lazy and good. With all of her extra time, Sarah had begun imagining Jake in her mind. She wanted to see him so badly. She couldn't wait until he was home and they could get back to their uncomplicated lives. She wanted to put this summer's events behind her.

Her mind also wandered to Samuel. She wasn't sure what her feelings were for this stranger who had invaded her life. She liked him -- no way could she deny this, but she didn't feel sure of him. What was going on with his family and that farm? She worried about him. She couldn't help feeling he was a victim of whatever was going on with his family and Gamble Farm. As if on cue, she heard the doorbell.

Joyce called Sarah to come into the living room. She came rushing into the room thinking Cassie had come back for a visit. She was surprised by the face she saw waiting for her. Sitting on the couch next to her mother was Samuel. He sat erect and proper as usual. She slowed her entrance and walked cautiously into the room taking a seat next to the couch. Should she be cautious of him? For whatever reason, she did not doubt Samuel. She was positive that he was as much a victim as she; although, the look on her mother's face said that not everyone was ready to dismiss Samuel's involvement in her kidnapping. It was evident that Joyce was struggling to maintain a friendly atmosphere toward Samuel. Unfortunately, Samuel realized this fact along with Sarah. He sat erect, but his facial expression gave away his defenselessness. He was well aware of Joyce's protective mother instinct.

Sarah knew she had to rescue him from her mother. She decided to get to the obvious questions everyone wanted to ask. "Samuel, I have a lot of questions that I can't answer about what happened to me the other day. I'm hoping you might fill in the gaps. Would you mind?"

Joyce leaned forward. Now was the time for answers. She was finally going to get information that would help her understand what was happening with Samuel and Sarah. She pushed away her need to ask Samuel questions thinking he would trust Sarah more and give her answers that he might not give to her.

Samuel hesitated for a moment, "I'll answer anything I can, Sarah. I'm not sure of how much help I will be but ask away," He sat back and focused on her as if looking at her would make him remember what had happened. He was trying desperately to keep his sight on Sarah and away from Joyce.

Sarah took a moment to look him over; she didn't know what to ask first or how to do so with her mother sitting in the room with them. Samuel knew she wouldn't ask him anything of significance with her mother there. He also knew that Joyce would make explaining things to Sarah impossible.

Sarah was aware that getting answers with her mother ready to pounce was impossible. She decided to try something. "Would you like to go out by the pool, Samuel? Mom and I have been sitting out there today, and it feels delightful."

Joyce wanted to shout 'No!', but held her tongue. She would honor Sarah's wishes. But she was determined to find out what was going on, and she wasn't going to wait much longer. She would discover what Samuel knew today before he left this house.

Samuel smoothly stood and offered Sarah to guide him out. The two made their way outside to the pool. She deliberately walked across the patio to the other side where the waterfall would drown out their voices from an overzealous, nosy mother.

Joyce kept her smile, but the fire hadn't died in her eyes. She had hoped to gather information from Sarah and Samuel's conversation to answer some of her questions about what had happened to her daughter and why. She watched as Sarah led their new neighbor to the pool area and noted that Samuel's eyes gave him away. He felt more for Sarah than just friends. She tried to determine what Sarah was feeling by her eyes, but she wasn't as visible as Samuel with her emotions.

The one thing Joyce had discovered was Samuel's feelings for her daughter. She believed that he would never hurt her. He cared for her. This fact was apparent. Her doubts about Samuel were subsiding. She filed them away for later reference if needed. For the moment, she studied the two's movements and their faces as they talked.

Sarah kept her smile for her mother's prying eyes. "Samuel, will you refresh my memory on the day of the attack. Did you come to help me when whatever attacked me?" She looked at him to see any indication of recognition of what she was saying. She only saw confusion.

"Sarah, I didn't know you'd been attacked until your mother called me that evening. We all met at your barns and began searching. Leigh and Mark, Josh and his parents along with Jake's family joined your parents. We searched without stopping until I found you in my bedroom."

Sarah looked at Samuel, "You have no idea of how or why I ended up at your home. I mean, why would someone take me to your house when I was so close to my home?" She pierced Samuel with her stare. She wanted answers, and she wanted Samuel to help her. Maybe he didn't know what was going on, but he had an idea; she felt sure.

Samuel looked at a loss for words. "I don't know what happened, Sarah. Please believe me. I was as scared as anyone -- maybe even more once I learned where you were when attacked."

Sarah studied Samuel. She believed him. He had never lied to her. He had been truthful to a fault. If he hadn't known about the attack, then who pulled the thing off her? Something or someone saved her. She had assumed it had been Samuel that had saved her. She told Samuel this, and he looked as if he was hurting.

"Sarah, I am so sorry I failed you. I never dreamed you would travel the ridge after all the times we discussed the dangers of traveling that trail. Why would you chance your safety? I should have kept better watch for you." He looked guilty and truly sorry.

Sarah moved close enough to touch Samuel's arm. "You're not the reason I was attacked, Samuel. You cannot and must not blame yourself."

Samuel grabbed her extended hand and squeezed. "You should not have to worry about getting attacked on your land. I feel like I've failed the community. I've tried to protect people around the farm, and I thought I had succeeded until you ended up in my bedroom injured. I am trying to decide what to do next to ensure everyone's safety."

Sarah stared at Samuel. Why did he think everyone's safety was his responsibility? When Samuel began answering her, she realized she had asked her question out loud. Samuel was stammering. Sarah was sure he was trying to answer her without giving up too much information. She held up her hand to stop him.

"Samuel, stop. Remember who I am? I am the person you have been using to keep everyone safe. I am not sure how or why you thought being my boyfriend would work, but apparently, you have reason to believe that having connections to the community would make us safe. I allowed this fake relationship to go on, and now you want to shoulder all of this yourself." Sarah fumed.

"Tell me, Samuel, what would have attacked me? You must know since you've been trying to protect me from whatever it might be. Why would I think it was you I caught a glimpse of before I lost consciousness? And, why was it you, I thought I saw standing in the bedroom the day before you said you were there? You stood at the foot of the bed without speaking to me. I am sure of it. Then you were gone, and the old guy took your place at the foot of the bed and stared at me. I am certain I saw the two of you sometime during my stay and then you came to rescue me."

Samuel reached over to Sarah's face and wiped the tear from her cheek. Sarah hadn't been aware that she had been crying. She was so tired of being confused. She wanted answers, and she wanted her life to go back to being ordinary and boring.

Samuel slumped over, staring at the concrete, battling within himself. "I hoped I wouldn't have to include you in on all of the sordid details. I'm going to tell you this, but you must promise me that we will be the only ones to know all of the truth about Gamble Farm. Do you promise me, Sarah?"

Sarah studied his face; he looked like a defenseless little boy trying to be brave and protective. His face scared her. This boy that had always carried a façade of calm and in control was completely out of control just under the surface.

"I'll try, Samuel. I can't promise you I'll keep silent. If Buffalo Creek needs to know this information I must tell them. I must protect the people that live on this creek. And, that lady in the window is anxiously waiting for answers to what you know about my attack." She and Samuel both turned to the window where Joyce stood looking out at them. They both waved at her, and she waved back but didn't move away from the window. She didn't care if they knew she was watching. As a matter of fact, she wanted them to know it was time to answer her questions, too.

Sarah smiled. "You do understand where I'm

coming from, don't you, Samuel?" she questioned.

She waited for a response from Samuel. He hesitated and took a deep breath before beginning. "I wouldn't endanger anyone Sarah; I've been trying to protect people here by keeping all of this horror to myself." He appeared lost and hurt when Sarah studied his face again. Her heart went out to him. He seemed to be this vulnerable little boy in an adult's body.

"Let me help you, Samuel." She reached for his arm. "Please, don't try to keep this to yourself anymore. You need help."

He smiled, "You're right, of course. I am not sure you are the person that needs to be helping me." He pulled her arms up to examine her gashes.

She felt very conscious of her wounds and pulled her arms away. "Telling me is the beginning to solving this--I can help you see things clearly. Maybe with the two of us, we can decide what we need to do next. Okay?" She waited for his response.

Samuel appeared to be struggling within himself once again. Sarah waited to see which side would win. Finally, he began to speak. "I'm not sure where to start." He stared at Sarah.

Without blinking, she returned his stare. "Start at the beginning. That is always a good place to begin." She smiled and waited.

Samuel cleared his throat to buy time. His stance gave way the fact that he hated to be telling this story. He dreaded Sarah's response after she heard what he had to say. Would she believe him? She had to believe him for her safety. He cleared his throat again and looked away from her.

"Sarah, this is one of the hardest things that I have ever done. Please believe me. I know that some of the things I am about to tell you are far-fetched, but you must believe that I am not making this up." He looked pleadingly at her face.

Sarah did believe him. "Samuel, I, of all people, understand how far-fetched this is. Remember, I'm the girl that was attacked and left locked up in your house for three days. Don't punish yourself any longer. Tell me what is going on, my friend."

The fact that she had just called him her friend wasn't lost on Samuel. He smiled, more to himself than at Sarah. He felt that they were friends. Through all that had happened, he had a friend. He didn't want to lose this friend. "Okay, here goes. Shall we sit down first? Telling this could take a while."

Sarah moved to the cushioned couch under the pergola, sitting down on one end so that Samuel had plenty of space to sit on the other end of the seat. Once they settled, she gave Samuel time to collect his thoughts and then prompted him to begin. "Start from the beginning. What made your parents come to Buffalo Creek, of all places, Samuel?"

Samuel looked deep into Sarah's soul. "Please hold your judgment until I have finished. Okay, friend?" He stressed the word friend as if reminding her of her acknowledgment of their friendship. She smiled and nodded in agreement. She sat quietly, bracing herself for what was to come.

Samuel turned away from Sarah's gaze and began to talk as if telling the wind the dreaded story. "I have always gone to a military school for boys until last year. During Thanksgiving break, I asked my parents if I might go to a public school for the experience. I told them I thought it would help me in real life, and since I was in high school now, it would be the optimal time to make the change. They were aghast at my request but agreed to think about the proposal.

"That was the last I heard of the request until I went back to Connecticut for Christmas break. Imagine my surprise to discover that my parents had bought me a farm in the foothills of Appalachia Kentucky. I wasn't sure what I would find here, but I was determined to make the best of the situation. I am not sure if my parents were punishing me or trying to fulfill my goal of learning to adapt to the world that surrounds me. Whichever the case, here I am."

Sarah interrupted, "Did they come with you? Why don't we ever see them around town?"

Samuel raised his hand, and with the expression on his face, Sarah knew she needed to sit quietly. It was clear that Samuel was in physical pain trying to tell this story. Asking questions and interrupting him was only making it more difficult for him. She settled back against the cushion of the seat and waited.

Samuel took a deep breath and pressed on with

his story. "My Christmas present was the Gamble Farm. I am not sure how they discovered this place, but I have my suspicions. I think my dad had his men find the least attractive and out of the way place for me to have and just like that, Gamble Farm became my home."

"That explains the men that encircled the farm when you first moved here." Sarah marveled, not realizing she had broken her vow to stay silent once again. She looked at Samuel and nodded her head at him, motioning him to go ahead with the story.

Samuel found himself laughing at this funny girl. He liked the way Sarah was an open book. Her thoughts and ideas were visible for all to see. Her obvious honesty is what he liked best about one who had become his only friend in the hollows of Kentucky.

He began his story again by answering Sarah's question. "My parents only came for a visit at the beginning of the move. I didn't lie when I said they had gone away on business. They stay in business mode and clearly can't do what they do here in the hollows of Buffalo Creek. And, before you ask, my father is in business, domestic and international, while Mom is a lawyer that deals only in large, profitable cases.

"They don't add up to much when it comes to being parents, but as professionals, they are the best at what they do. I am an only child. I guess they decided once I came along that parenting didn't suit them, so they shipped me off to be raised by school personnel and teachers while they did what they do best. They have given me anything I asked for except for parents; this they couldn't afford."

Sarah wanted to cradle him and shield him from his life. How sad he seemed at this moment. No wonder he didn't like talking about his family. He didn't have a family. He truly was alone in the world. She refrained from speaking, and she resisted taking his hand to support him through the story. She sat waiting to hear more.

Samuel continued, "Once, they visited and saw where I would be living; they ordered the fence and the rebuilding of the property and buildings. When the carpenters and other workers began the renovations, they left for Connecticut, and I was alone.

"I have lived alone on the farm with all the workers since that time.

I must say it was great until about two weeks after I moved into the house. I had the responsibilities I had longed for and the freedom to explore the beautiful land surrounding the farm. On one of those explorations, I met you and your friends."

He looked at Sarah and smiled. She smiled back at him but didn't speak. She wanted to hear more. He didn't disappoint. "About two weeks after I had moved into the house, I was getting ready for bed when I felt a cold chill sweep through the house. It was so strong that I was certain that one of the workers or I had left the front door open. When I went into the entry, I found the door closed and locked. Where the freezing air was coming from, I didn't know. After checking all the doors and windows downstairs, I ruled out that outside air was coming inside. I started back upstairs to go to bed when I heard a loud, disturbing sound from the kitchen. I ran toward the sound, not knowing who was in my house yet all I found was my kitchen in complete disarray. I couldn't believe that anyone would do this to my house.

"There in front of me, anything that was not nailed down was scattered all over the floor. I left the mess for the maid to clean the next day and started back upstairs to go to bed. I didn't make it up the stairs. About half way up I felt a strong kick to my ribs. It knocked the breath out of me. While I tried to regain my breathing, I felt someone push me over and over again. I held on to the stair railing. I knew that someone or something was trying to kill me. I ran the rest of the way up the stairs to my bedroom trying to wrap my brain around what was happening to me. I was scared for my life."

He hesitated while studying Sarah's face for her reaction. He whispered, "There hadn't been anyone on the stairwell with me, and yet I had the bruises to prove that my mind wasn't playing tricks on me. I didn't know what to do. The next day I asked the workers if they had seen anyone around the house, but no one had been near the house all evening."

"After that, I asked the maid to take a downstairs bedroom, just so someone other than me would be in the house. I hoped since no one had mentioned any peculiar happenings it was a one-time thing and if I weren't alone it would be deterred from occurring again." The look on Samuel's face gave way to how much fear he had felt during the incident. His tired eyes clouded with the fear that he must have felt that night. Sarah knew how he felt; she had felt the same thing only days ago.

She couldn't resist, "Samuel, that is exactly how I felt the other day. Why didn't you tell me you had experienced the same thing?" She searched his face for answers.

Samuel dismissed her question and continued with his story. "Things were quiet for a while. Then Mrs. Bellows, the maid, came to me after I got home from school one day. She was white as a sheet. She said she refused to stay in the house alone and would be leaving by the end of the week. When I asked her what had made her feel this way she only shook her head at me and told me to leave.

"She didn't make it to the end of the week. She left the next day for the Lexington Airport. I guess I'll never know what frightened her so badly, but I can guess. My parents sent another man to help out around the house, Mr. Sparks. He still works for me, but he has his quarters out back of the main house. He insisted. Since Mrs. Bellows left, I stay in the main house alone."

Samuel paused to allow Sarah time to digest what he was revealing to her. He stared at her face for a moment and then looked away and spoke as if he were talking with an invisible person. "Right before I came to get you to help with keeping everyone safe I had another visitor. This time, it showed itself or at least a form of itself."

He turned to watch Sarah's reaction to what he was going to say to her next. "A white-haired, rickety, old man walked in front of my TV one evening." Samuel released a hollow laugh, "Just as if it was as common and normal as anything."

Samuel's voice shook, "I felt fear begin to take control of me. I was so scared that my bones hurt. I couldn't move, let alone speak. I just sat there waiting. The old man stared at me for what seemed a very long time and then he spoke. His voice sounded brittle as if I could reach out and snap it in the air. He told me that I must bring a wife into the house. He had chosen the one on the ridge to be the mistress of the house. I knew he meant you. I found myself asking him to wait until I had courted you properly. Samuel stressed the turn of phrase he'd used with the appration. He agreed to wait, but that I must make you Mistress of Gamble Farm. He turned and moved from the TV and disappeared into nothingness." Samuel reached his hand out and grabbed the empty air in front of him. He shrugged his shoulder and went on.

"I sat there wondering what to do. I knew this thing could be violent, and I could not allow it to release its wrath on you or your friends." He dropped his head, staring down at the water moving in the pool. "So my plans to go back home to my parents' house was forgotten, and I came to you the next day. I had to protect you, Sarah. I had to do whatever it took to make sure everyone was safe." Samuel looked at Sarah and smiled, but the smile didn't reach his eyes. "You know the rest of that story." He looked sheepishly over at Sarah.

Sarah tried to absorb all that Samuel was telling her. That is why you had to act like we were dating. Did having a fight with me work? Well, I guess not since I was attacked shortly after the big fight."

Samuel gave her a moment to process the story so far and then picked up where he left off, "After your incident, I decided it was time that I do some research on this thing haunting my house. I need to know what it is and how to get rid of it. I can't allow it to do to the community what it did to you." Samuel's face turned white. "Or God forbid, have something else happen to you." Samuel allowed his eyes to settle on Sarah for a long moment before continuing.

"So, I visited the library in town to discover there was nothing there that could help me. The next day I drove to Lexington hoping that the University of Kentucky's library would offer some answers." Samuel saw Sarah's expression of hope and he shook his head in defeat. "I wish I could report that I solved all our problems, but that isn't true. I found a few bits of information that are helpful in understanding what's going on; I didn't find enough to act on this thing."

Samuel drifted into a conversation almost with himself, "I'm fearful of what it will do to the community if I don't get the wall completed. From the small bit, I discovered, I think we can contain the spirit to the farm if we have that rock wall surrounding the farm. I guess that the wall is what disturbed him. He appeared once the building of the wall began. Maybe we disturbed his final resting place or something when we started digging the foundation for the wall." Samuel seemed to be in his own world but quickly shook his head as if to clear his thoughts. "So, what started out as something to help in renovating the farm released this spirit and if I'm right, it's the thing that will keep the spirit contained to the farm.

"The workers keep trying to finish, but something keeps happening to delay them. Of course, I have my suspicions as to why that is occurring. I keep asking the workers if they have seen anything unusual, and all I get is that they haven't seen anything, but plenty of odd things have happened.

"They blame each other for the incidents and don't give credit to anything supernatural as the culprit. I'm just as happy that they don't think in this manner. I'm counting on them not to think in this manner. That way they won't quit working, and that wall will get finished."

Sarah wrinkled her forehead, "Why is the wall so important?"

Samuel kept going as if he stopped he couldn't finish. It was almost like he didn't know Sarah was sitting beside him. He was in his world, and he was finally getting out what he had kept secret from others until now. He was releasing the torture that he had been living with this summer. "One of the things I discovered at the library in Lexington was that this thing or the apparition might be contained when its home is encircled by a wall of limestone. So, I asked that limestone be added to build the wall around the farm."

Sarah blurted out before thinking, "Isn't that expensive? I mean really expensive?"

Samuel looked at her for the first time in a long time and commented, "My parents have money, Sarah. They don't care how much money I spend on this land. They figure once I'm finished with my adventure they can sell the farm at a profit. They don't realize that the value of money here is different from the value of the dollar in Connecticut or New York."

Sarah glanced down at Samuel's clinched hands. He was trying very hard to keep from shaking. He was apparently torn up because of what he had lived through this summer. She couldn't help but reach out and put her steady hand on top of his. He relaxed under the warmth of her hand.

"Once we had our fight, I hoped that the apparition would realize that we were not compatible and would leave you and me alone. At least, I hoped I could keep it at bay until I discovered more information that would help me contain it or get rid of it permanently. I was wrong. He came after me with a vengeance."

"I was in my bedroom the evening you were attacked when my door slammed shut. When I tried to open it, I was pushed to the floor and slung from one side of the room to the other side. I found myself pushed up against the wall although I saw nothing that was doing this to me. I lost consciousness, and the next thing I knew was the phone ringing, and your mother asking me if I had seen you."

Samuel looked deeply into Sarah's eyes and declared, "If anything had happened to you I would have lost it, Sarah. I couldn't bear to have you hurt because of this."

He began again, "After talking with your mom, I checked my bedroom and the door and all was as if nothing had happened except for my sore ribs. I rushed to meet your parents and the neighbors, and we began scouring the hills hunting for you. Cassie's horse had made its way to the barn, and everyone was worried that you had fallen off and gotten hurt. I didn't tell anyone of my suspicions. I hoped I was wrong and even so, who would believe me?"

"We searched for days and then we all decided to get some food and sleep for an hour before beginning again. When I entered my house that day, I heard moaning from the downstairs bedroom. Imagine my surprise and fear when I discovered you lying on my bed. I had never been as frightened as when I discovered you in my house in my entire life. All I could think of was getting you out safely. I was scared the apparition would discover us, and we would both be in grave danger. Luckily, we made it to your house, and all is well."

Sarah interrupted once again, "Samuel, tell me you didn't go back to that house that night." She searched for an answer, but only got an almost guilty smile from him.

"How could you go back into that danger? Why would you do that to yourself?" She scolded him.

Samuel dismissed her scolding and continued with the story, "Things have been fine, except for the first time I entered after taking you home. The old man showed his presence again. He warned me that the only way you and I could live would be together in the house."

Samuel's dark eyes pierced Sarah, "He meant it, Sarah. He felt our connection when I rescued you and allowed us to leave. I thought we had tricked him and escaped, but I know he allowed us to leave. He thinks we are connected and that we will be together in the house, or we wouldn't be here now. We have to find a way out of this before it's too late, Sarah. I know Jake is due home soon. I fear for us all when he returns, and it's obvious what your feelings are for him."

Sarah felt that she had enough information to offer her thoughts. "Is the wall fence completed?"

Samuel nodded his head and confirmed, "It should be finished this afternoon or no later than tomorrow. That means that if what I have read is true, the apparition will at least be contained to inside the wall if the fence stays a complete circle. No one can leave the fence open, or the circle is broken. Just the workers or I going in or out could allow it to escape."

"Samuel, you must stay here with my family until this is over. You can't risk your safety in that place," Sarah declared.

Samuel's refusal was adamant, "If I don't go back, he will come after me, Sarah. That means your family, your neighbors, your friends, and you will be in danger. I cannot allow that to happen. I refuse to allow this danger to hurt the place I hope to call my home for a long time to come."

Sarah smiled, "You really want to stay in Salyersville? You want to make this your home even after all of this?"

Samuel smiled, "I love this little town, believe it or not. The people have been so friendly, almost like family. I want this in my life."

Sarah straightened her shoulders as if readying herself for battle, "Then we need to take care of this and get on with our lives. Shall we get started, my friend?"

Samuel wasn't ready to put a happy twist to this just yet. "I'm doing all I know to do. I know what it is that exists on my farm, I just don't know how to get rid of it. I have to do more research on the apparition. I plan on going back to Lexington tomorrow. Hopefully, I can find out either how to take care of this thing or know who can help me to get rid of it." His frown lines deepened as he thought of the challenge in front of him.

Sarah absentmindedly stared at the pool. Once she had made sense of her thoughts she reasoned out loud. "Samuel, when I was locked up in your bedroom I saw you standing in front of the bed, but it was an older you. You could have been middle-aged from your appearance. Since you didn't come to the farm during my time in the bedroom, we can surmise that something has taken on your appearance."

She drifted off into silence once again. Samuel sat waiting for her to make sense of her thoughts. He was patient on the outside, although he wanted to scream for her to get to the point. Sarah's face was set in a frown as her thoughts took shape.

"Samuel, do you remember Mammy's reaction to you when we visited her? She acted as if she'd seen a ghost. She said you looked like an old beau of hers. Do you remember?"

Samuel nodded. "Yes, at first I thought I'd have to leave because she was upset. Then, after her initial reaction to me, she seemed to like me." Samuel smiled at the memory.

Sarah nodded. "I think we need to visit Mammy. She might be able to help us with what or who is terrorizing your farm. Last year she helped Cassie and Josh identify the lady ghost at Cassie's house. Mammy is a wealth of history when it comes to Lick Creek and Buffalo Creek."

Samuel's face showed the fear he felt for Sarah's idea. "Sarah, we can't endanger Mammy. What if it knows why we're visiting Mammy and we cause harm to her?"

Sarah nodded. "I agree we have to protect Mammy, but what if Josh invites us to visit with her for lunch? We visit her all the time so it wouldn't be suspicious."

Samuel fought the urge to pace around the pool. He wanted to protect everyone and keep this horrific being away from the community. Sarah was suggesting they include Josh and Mammy on the issues of his farm.

Sarah didn't give him time to decline her suggestion. "We can tell Josh that you are trying to find out the history of your farm and who better to tell you about the farm than Mammy? That way Josh and Mammy will be protected from what is happening."

Samuel was shaking his head in refusal. He wasn't ready to endanger anyone else that wasn't already involved. He desperately wanted to protect his neighbors.

Sarah found Samuel's eyes with her own and leveled her gaze. "Samuel, how long do you think this thing will stay put before venturing off the farm. We will none be safe then. We must find out what it is if we are going to conquer it."

Slowly, Samuel agreed. Sarah didn't give him time to back out from his agreement. She pulled her phone out of her pocket and called Josh. "Hi, Josh. How's it going at your place?" She frowned. "I'm feeling ok. I need a break from being lazy at home all day every day. What do you think about a visit to Mammy's?"

She smiled, "Great." She hesitated and then added, "And Josh, Samuel wants to join us. He is wondering about the history of his farm and I told him that Mammy would be the person that could tell him."

She paused, frowned and added, "Josh, Samuel is one of us. He has no idea of what happened to me. Believe me; I would know if he did."

She stole a glance at Samuel. This moment was one of those rare moments that the real Samuel broke through the façade. She wasn't sure if he was distressed because of the visit, or that Josh questioned his friendship with her. All she knew was that this hard, formal young man was hurting, and he needed friends to help him through this ordeal.

"Okay, Josh. I'll tell Samuel, and we can meet you tomorrow at your house." She finished the call and held Samuel's hand. "This is the right thing to do

Samuel. We'll be careful."

Samuel nodded, not certain that he believed Sarah. What he did know was that he needed help and Mammy might be the missing link to this puzzle so he would go along with Sarah's idea. He prayed that Sarah, Josh, and Mammy would be safe.

"I hope you know what you are doing, Sarah. What time do you want me to pick you up tomorrow?"

Sarah began declining the ride offer, but Samuel held up his hand to stop her refusal. "If we are doing this we have to keep the apparition at bay. If he sees us together, he is more apt to relax. So, what time do you want me to pick you up tomorrow?"

Sarah relented, "Five o'clock will be okay. We will get to Josh's by 5:30 and to Mammy's in time for dinner. We'll have a nice chat and then back home. It will be a regular day. Nothing out of the ordinary."

"Okay, we can talk with Mammy and then I'll visit the library in Lexington again. Maybe Mammy will give me something to help solve the puzzle." He stared at his hands. "I hope we are doing the right thing, Sarah."

"That's a good plan. We'll pump Mammy for information and then search the library for more answers later." Sarah was eager to begin.

Samuel released a growl of a laugh. "What do you mean we will pump Mammy, and then we will go to Lexington? You can't get in danger's way, Sarah. I can't allow you to get too close to this. Look at what it's done to you already." He gestured toward her arms. "Granted, Josh will expect you to be with me to visit Mammy, but you can't risk going to Lexington. You have been through enough."

Sarah looked at Samuel, "Okay, the apparition will expect us to be together, right? So, I am going with you. I feel strong enough to ride in a car, and I can help you with your research. Don't argue with me; I'm going. Now, let's persuade my parents that I need to get out of the house and that a visit with Mammy is just what I need. I can convince them that a ride to Lexington with you is just what the doctor ordered. I'll tell them I need to get away from Buffalo to clear my head. It'll work."

Sarah thought of the guilt Samuel had put on himself because of this thing on the farm which he had bought. She wanted him to know that he wasn't the only person on the Creek with this kind of trouble. She caressed his hand and leaned into him as if telling him a secret. "And Samuel, your farm isn't the only farm around here that has disturbing paranormal happenings. Leigh and Cassie have had several incidents at their house. Theirs isn't as vicious as yours, but they still have sightings. So don't feel like you'll be run out of town for experiencing such things." She gazed unseeingly at the blue water in the pool.

"We kind of know why Leigh and Cassie have their lady of the house. I wonder why your apparition has shown up now. We've been going to that farm forever and hanging out there, and I've never seen or heard anything strange. I wonder what happened to bring this thing to the farm when you finally began to make it livable again?"

"I don't know. The first time I saw the apparition was on the stairs at home," Samuel mumbled deep in thought. "You know, the first few weeks I was on the farm, I didn't see anything unusual. It was just an old run down farmhouse." He looked out over the lawn, "What changed? What was different after the first couple of weeks? I was living in the house all that time, and nothing happened." He pondered to himself.

Sarah didn't notice much of what Samuel was saying. She had stopped listening when she heard Samuel question when the unusual happenings began occurring. She, along with Samuel, was deep in thought. She kept thinking of the events that had happened this summer. She had an idea. She turned to Samuel. "Samuel, when did the renovations on the farm begin? Did they start before the apparition showed himself?

Samuel thought for a moment before answering. "The first time I saw the old man was the day after we began the major renovations to the farmhouse. You have to realize that we had several crews working around the clock to get the place in working order. A lot of changes were done in a few day's time." His eyes widened. "Sarah, do you think that I have brought this thing here because of the demolition I've done on the farm?"

"I don't know, but it would explain many of the

things that have happened to you and me." Sarah studied Samuel's face for a reaction to what she was saying. Samuel was obviously listening intently to her every word. His eyes pierced her own as she spoke. "I know that things happen, I mean paranormal things." Sarah hesitated, "Leigh and Cassie have learned to live with paranormal happenings. Occasionally, the woman entity that lingers in their home allows them to see her." Sarah stopped to check Samuel's reaction once again. Samuel was giving Sarah all of his attention. It was as if he thought that if he took his eyes away from Sarah, he would miss something important. Sarah felt her heart ache for this boy that seemed so lost at this moment. She half smiled, "After a while, they discovered that the entity wasn't going to harm them, and they learned to live together." She shrugged her shoulders.

Samuel looked at Sarah with disbelief. "I can't believe we are discussing this in a serious manner. I don't or didn't until now, believe in paranormal beings. I guess there has to be an explanation for what is going on, and this seems to be the most reasonable answer. I can't believe I just said this was a reasonable explanation." They both laughed at the situation. It was a laugh etched with anxiety.

He stood up and took Sarah's hand and pulled. "So, you want to go researching with me this week? It's going to be a long day. It takes two hours just to drive to Lexington. The searching takes time and then we have to drive two hours back. You have just gone through a rough time. Are you sure you're ready for such a full day?"

Sarah smiled, "I can't think of anything that would be better for me than to go searching for a way out of a situation that has entangled us. It would be the best medicine for me."

Samuel smiled, "Don't you think we need to get permission from your parents first? I still see your mom standing guard at the window. How are we going to explain this without explaining this?"

Sarah smiled and waved at her mother. Joyce waved back but didn't lose her serious face as she stared at the two. "Okay, we have to tell her something. What can we give her that will satisfy her for the moment?"

She thought about the situation and came up

with a partial truth. "You follow my lead, Samuel. I think I can get the suspicions off of you."

Samuel looked at Sarah not quite believing she could pull it off but willing to try. "If you pull this off, and they agree, I'll pick you up around 8 o'clock, day after tomorrow?"

"Oh, I can get permission. Just sit back and watch," Sarah giggled.

She led Samuel back into the living room where her mom and dad were pretending to watch the evening news. "Mom, Dad; Samuel and I have been discussing my attack, and we are confident that there has to be a connection to the rehabbing of Samuel's farm and the old man that I saw. Samuel says that there are several workers and it's hard to distinguish the man from the other workers since they are all older. He's keeping an eye out for anyone who looks like my description and will sneak a picture of him and send it to me to identify him." Sarah stopped and looked at her parents to see if her explanation worked. From the relief on both her parents' faces, she knew that her plan worked perfectly.

She didn't want to lose her momentum, so she plunged on with her request. "Since I've been sitting here day in and day out healing, I think I need to get out and clear my mind to recuperate from the stress I'm feeling. So, I want to ask your permission for something. I want to remind you that I need to get out of here to recuperate from the emotional side of this thing that happened to me." She paused long enough to get her breath. "I talked to Josh, and he invited Samuel and me to visit with Mammy tomorrow. I think a visit with Mammy will work wonders for me."

Joyce and Dan both agreed that going to Mammy's would be the first step in recovery. "I think Mammy's apple pie is the very thing you need. So, Josh is going with you?" Joyce wasn't completely satisfied with Samuel's innocence yet.

Sarah smiled. "Yes, you know he wouldn't miss one of Mammy's spreads for anything. He will meet us at his house, and we will all go over together."

Joyce was still feeling an uneasiness with Samuel and Sarah together. Dan saw his wife struggling with giving up her protective shield over her daughter. He had to help her move forward. "Okay, but you two need to call us when you get there and when you start home. You never know if that old man will show up again. We want you to be alert. And that goes for you too, Samuel. If he is lurking around your farm, you have to be careful."

Samuel agreed wholeheartedly.

Sarah decided she might as well jump in with the rest of the plan. She smiled at both of her parents to prepare them for more to come. "Samuel has invited me to ride down to Lexington with him later this week. I think it is what I need. I can clear my head and forget this ordeal for a while. May I please go? I might get to see Jake on campus since Samuel is going to the library there."

At first, Joyce was livid at the proposition. She could barely allow her daughter to leave the house to visit an old friend let alone travel two hours away from home with a boy that might be responsible for her kidnapping. She hardly ever refused her daughter, but this was insane. Sarah was not thinking clearly. Joyce's first reaction was, "Absolutely not."

That was all she could get out. She refused even

to consider a trip with Samuel. Dan, on the other hand, knew that if Sarah was going to recover fully without scares from this horrible experience, she needed to get back to normal activity as soon as possible.

Sarah was grateful for her father's level head. Once he discussed his theory, Joyce finally agreed that Sarah could ride to Lexington with Samuel. She was not happy with the plans to travel two hours to Lexington. But finally, she relented.

Sarah hugged her mother and then her father whispering "thank you, Daddy." She knew when to leave well enough alone. She signaled Samuel to leave, and he took the hint. "Well, I'll leave you to rest, Sarah. I'm so glad you are feeling better. I'm on my way to do some investigating at the farm. I'll send you pictures of anyone that matches the description of the old man.

TWENTY

Joyce went to work the next day, promising to be home in time to have lunch with Sarah. True to her word, at noon she was home with Subway sandwiches for the both of them. She had found it hard to stay away from her daughter. She had a long talk with herself. She knew if she kept treating Sarah as injured she would become part of the problem. She wanted her daughter to heal and be normal again. She decided she would send Sarah to Mammy's for the afternoon and then she would send her to Lexington. She vowed to do so without allowing Sarah to know how frightened she was for her.

At five o'clock Sarah sat by the front door waiting for Samuel. She was eager to have sometime away from the trouble that plagued her peaceful, comfortable world. Mammy would be a delight to visit. Samuel pulled in the driveway exactly at 5 o'clock in typical Samuel style. She called to her mom announcing that she was leaving and off she ran to meet Samuel. She had to admit that she liked being around Samuel. She felt comfortable with him. They had become close friends through all of the eerie happenings of the summer.

They drove over to Josh's and found him waiting on his porch. He leaped from the porch and climbed in the BMW. After some maneuvering of Josh's legs, they were off to Mammy's. During the ride over Josh entertained them with Mammy's menu of the day.

Mammy met the teens at the door. The aroma of her cooked goodies pulled them into the house. Josh didn't waste anytime in finding the dining room table. As an afterthought he invited Samuel and Sarah to join him. They all laughed. Josh was like a kid on Christmas morning.

Mammy's beady eyes locked on Samuel again. She tried to act naturally but Sarah caught her staring at Samuel at any given time during the visit. Samuel didn't seem to be uncomfortable with her persistent staring.

After getting his belly full, Josh told Mammy the reason for their visit. "Mammy, Samuel here is wanting to know some history about his new farm. We told him you were the person that could tell him about it if anyone could.

Mammy patted Josh's back. "You know I've been here longer than anyone else. I can remember your farm back before Jed and Susan Gamble lived there." Mammy got a faraway look as if she was going back to a time when the Gamble Farm was owned by different owners. "I have to say that before the Gamble's the farm wasn't a very happy place. I remember that the couple that lived there only had two sons. The husband's father lived with them too. It was hard for the small family to make a go of it. They worked hard but couldn't seem to get ahead of the game."

Mammy smiled. "Samuel, do you remember the first time you came to visit me?"

Samuel nodded his head.

"Well, you see, one of the son's that lived on your farm and you look like twins. I can't look at you now without seeing my Sam. You look so much like him." Mammy didn't hide her examination of Samuel. She leaned in toward Samuel as he stuffed fried potatoes into his mouth. "You even have the same mannerisms as Sam." She shook her head. "It's remarkable."

"What was their last name, Mammy?" Sarah quizzed.

"Sam's last name was Lykins. His brother's name was Palmer. The husband and wife were Bernice and Tom Lykins. The old man, Tom's daddy was ornery. He was always a mean one. I remember Sam always being scared of his grandpa. I believe his name was Henry."

"Do you know any juicy stories about the family? Anything that happened while they lived at the farm?" Sarah pressed. She was determined to find out anything she could about the farm.

Mammy laughed a hollow laugh. It wasn't a jolly laugh she always had when they came to visit. She seemed sad. "Funny you should ask. There is definitely a story to tell. I'm sorry to say that it wasn't a happy one."

Mammy looked around the room at the young faces. "Sam was about your age. His brother Palmer was only a baby. The Lykins family had tried and tried to have more children but after Sam, they didn't have any more until Palmer."

"Back then people had children to work the fields and to help keep the farm going. The grandfather belittled his son all the time about not having children. He spoke to the wife horribly. He called her names and rumors were that he beat her up on occasion. I'm not sure what the husband did or if he did anything until that one night."

Mammy wiped a tear from her wrinkled cheek. "No one knows for sure what actually happened, but people talked. I just know what the end results were. When the fight was finished, Sam and Tom were both shot and killed. Henry was in the house with a gun in his hand. The story was told that the old man lost his temper and killed his son and then Sam tried to take the gun from his grandfather and was shot. The old man couldn't bare what he had done so he shot himself. Funny thing is that after that night Bernice and baby Palmer were never seen in Salyersville again."

Mammy stared out the window. "Sam and I were sweet on each other at the time it happened. I thought he was the prettiest thing I ever saw. He was such a good boy. I had made up my mind that he was the one. I planned on marrying that boy." She allowed a long breath to escape.

Then she perked up, "But, then, I met Josh's great-grandpa. He was the apple of my eye, and we lived a good life." She smiled. "Life is uncertain. You take what you get. God was good to me. My Jeb was a good man. I've had a good life."

Mammy shook her head as if to free her of the past. "After the Lykins family was gone, the county sold the farm to the Gamble family on the courthouse steps. They had a large family and lived there until the children left and they died."

Josh was the first to speak. "Wow, Mammy. I had no idea you had another beau other than Grandpa."

Mammy's old eyes danced. "I was a looker in the day. I know it don't show now, but the boys were lined up to court me." She laughed a genuine laugh this time.

She pulled her body close to Samuel so she could get a good look at him. I hope I didn't give you too much information. It's been a good farm since all that happened. The Gamble's raised their family on the land. They seemed to be happy; at least until all their kids left town. They left out one by one. They lived the last of their lives alone in that house."

Samuel reached for Mammy's old crinkled hand. He held her hand and sincerely thanked her. "Mammy, I want to thank you for the information about my home. I know this hasn't been easy for you to discuss with us – especially about Sam.

Mammy didn't miss a beat, "My Goodness, you look just like him. It's amazing.

She put her other hand over Samuel's and her hands and pulled herself back to the present. "Now, enough of going back to the past. We are here in the present, and I've cooked all this food. You guys have to eat up."

They all followed orders and ate until they all

three were stuffed. Sarah stopped after one piece of pie. She and Mammy watched as Josh and Samuel gobbled down all of the food on the table.

Sarah giggled. "We won't be able to fit into Samuel's car if you two don't stop eating."

Samuel was the first to give. He held his stomach and vowed not to take another bite until the next week. Josh held his stomach but didn't pretend that he wouldn't be eating for a while. He was known to pop in on his Mammy and find leftovers to munch on while working in the fields.

Sarah used Mammy's phone to alert her parents that she was on her way home. After her call, the three hugged and thanked Mammy. They all promised to come back soon. They wobbled out of the house and climbed in the BMW waving at a happy Mammy as they left.

Josh was the first to address the Gamble Farm's history. "Can you believe that this little community has such a colorful history? I mean, we never have anything happen these days. Not that I want to have killings going on in our neighborhood."

He pulled up to sit so he was close to the front seat. "Samuel, sounds like your farm has a history. Maybe more than you wanted."

Samuel nodded. "It definitely has a story to go along with it, doesn't it? He looked at Sarah and laughed the dry fake laugh he used when he wanted to keep his emotions under control.

When they dropped Josh at his house, Samuel looked at Sarah. "Can you believe what Mammy told us? How did she know all the names of the people in my family?

Sarah was slow in connecting all the names. "I know that Mammy's beau has your name but what other names are similar?"

Samuel looked pale, "My father's name is Palmer, and my Grandmother is Bernie."

The two of them were at a loss for words. They wanted puzzle pieces to help them solve this mystery, and they got some really huge pieces.

Sarah said goodnight to Samuel and numbly went in her house still stunned from the visit with

Mammy.

TWENTY-ONE

The next morning at eight o'clock sharp Samuel's red BMW pulled into the driveway. Joyce met Sarah on the stairs. "Honey, I'm not sure that this is a good idea. The more I think about it, the more I question it."

Sarah refused to give in to her mother's concerns. "Mom, I know Samuel. He is going to be just what I need. I need a friend I can relax with and forget what has happened." She looked at her mother with her most persuasive eyes. "Please, don't keep me here."

Dan met the two by the door, "You be careful and keep us posted on what is happening." His face gave way his concern.

Sarah began reasoning with them on why this was a good idea when the doorbell rang. Samuel stepped into the entry. Sarah dreaded what was sure to happen next. She wasn't sure that Samuel was up to the interrogation her parents would certainly dish out at him.

Joyce didn't miss a beat, "Good morning, Samuel. I'm glad you came inside. I have concerns about this trip. What exactly are the two of you going to be doing? You know how weak Sarah is at the moment."

Samuel nodded. "I know the fragile state she is in, and that is why I think this day trip will be like therapy for her. We can drive leisurely to Lexington and visit the library. I'll do the research, and if I notice her getting tired, I'll insist she stop and rest. Should anything cause me or her to be alarmed, I'll bring her home as soon as I can get her here. I'll make sure we call you every hour to report what's happening. I promise to protect her with my life."

Sarah looked at Samuel's face. Wow, she was sure he meant every word he was saying. Apparently, her parents believed it too because they said their "goodbyes" and the friends were on their way. They bound out of the door and for the first time in weeks Sarah felt light-footed as she ran to the car. Once seated, she greeted Samuel with a broad smile that reached her eyes.

Samuel was sure he hadn't seen her look as beautiful as she did this morning. He had to check himself. He didn't want Sarah to feel that she couldn't be comfortable around him. He knew she was Jake's girlfriend and probably would be for a long time to come. He felt a bit of jealousy run through his core but found it easy to push away when Sarah hopped in the car and beamingly announced, "It's a beautiful morning to be going for a drive. Thanks for allowing me to go with you. I feel wonderful to be getting away from here for a day."

Samuel smiled back at her and replied, "I'm looking forward to getting away myself. I think I am getting the better end of the deal. I've gained an able-bodied assistant to help with the research."

Samuel noticed the slight frown that touched Sarah's face as she rubbed her injured arms. He frowned himself. He had meant to keep the conversation light but mistakenly tread into a worrisome conversation. "I'm sorry Sarah; I didn't mean to spoil our good mood."

Sarah's face became cloudy as she blurted out, "Samuel, how was your night? Was it quiet on the farm? I hate that you have to stay at that place." She stopped and waited for Samuel's answer.

He looked at her with a half grin on his face. "You do get riled up, don't you, Miss Sarah Arnett?" He took time for a long hard laugh. Then he turned to her questions. "The night was very peaceful. I didn't hear or see anything or anyone. The workers are hard at work finishing the fence today. It should be completed when we return this evening."

"I spent most of the night thinking about Mammy's story. I can't get the fact that the people that lived in my home before me had the same names as my family and me. She said that one of them even looked like me. You know how she gets when I show up to visit."

Sarah agreed with Samuel. "I know; I couldn't go to sleep because I couldn't get Mammy's voice out of my head." She stopped and watched the scenery pass by as they rode down the highway. "I think we need to search for information on the Lykins family from Salyersville."

Samuel's face became serious, "Do you think we will find anything about the family all the way down in Lexington? I think we might find something in Frankfort, the capital." He shrugged, "It won't hurt to try."

He turned onto the main highway and sped toward the strip of town that had a choice of Dairy Queen, McDonald's or a mom and pop place called The Appalachian Restaurant. "Are you up for some breakfast before we get started?" He had already pulled into the parking lot of The Appalachian Restaurant. Sarah hadn't eaten much since her incident, but today she felt like she could eat a horse if put in front of her.

"I think I could stand to have a few pancakes. How about you?" She flashed her teasing smile.

"That sounds magnificent. I think blueberry would be delicious." He rubbed his stomach as he jumped out of his car. Sarah didn't wait for his help; she jumped out and followed alongside him. They had pancakes and coffee. When they were leaving, they each took an extra cup of coffee as they headed back on the road.

The drive to Lexington went by quickly. It seemed they just started out of the driveway when Samuel pulled into the library parking lot near the University of Kentucky campus. Sarah peered out the window at her surroundings. "So this is where Jake has spent his summer."

It looked large with too many people moving around like bees near a flower garden. Some were walking; some rode bikes and some were on skateboards. They moved fast like they were all on different missions, but everyone's mission was just as important as another.

Sarah watched as groups of students gathered to talk and laugh or to study or just to hang out while listening to their iPods. She wondered if Jake ever hung out in these spots or maybe even with these people. She wished she could look through the groups and see Jake laughing or studying with the rest of the students.

Sarah smiled to herself. If she saw him, she would walk up and join in just to see the look on his face. She longed to see him again. It seemed like it had been so long since they said goodbye to each other. In only a week, their summer apart would be finished, and they could get back to normal. Most every one of the gang had made it back to Salyersville. Most had either called or sent word that they wanted to help her in any way they could.

Logan and Seth were ready to go hunting for whatever attacked her. She scolded the both of them and dared them not to go into the woods. They both finally promised to abide by her wishes, but they were ready any time she could be persuaded to change her mind.

She neglected to tell them about Samuel's connection to the strange happenings. She wanted Samuel to become a part of the gang. He was one of the nicest people she knew, and if the guys could just have time to see past his stern, stuffy façade, they would welcome him into their gang and their community.

Samuel couldn't control the apparition that was plaguing the community and endangering the entire neighborhood. Actually, without Samuel, there probably would be more incidents than just Sarah's.

She stole a quick glance at Samuel as they walked up the large marble stairs to the entrance of the library. He looked tense. Apparently, he was back to thinking of what to do to make the neighborhood safe from whatever was loose on his farm. His businesslike manner encouraged Sarah to become motivated to working diligently.

They searched every mode available in the library. They searched periodicals, paranormal magazines, books on any subject that might lead to paranormal incidents. They worked their way through the first half of the day when Samuel found Sarah in the computer lab.

"I'm starved! My brain is shutting down. I think I need a change of scenery. Let's get a bite to eat and regroup. There's an Olive Garden up the street. What do you think?"

Sarah had been so involved in her reading that she hadn't thought about food. Her stomach was telling her that it agreed with Samuel. She didn't want to waste a moment in finding a solution to their problem, but one look at Samuel and she knew that he had already made up his mind. They were going for food. "Okay, you've twisted my arm or persuaded my stomach, let's go. I love the Olive Garden."

While they waited on their pasta, she asked Samuel about his findings. She could tell by the dark shade of his eyes that he hadn't had any luck. She hadn't found anything that would help either. They tried not to allow the failure of the morning influence their motivation for the afternoon. Just as they were finishing their food and getting ready to leave, Sarah heard her name.

Surely someone else in the restaurant was named Sarah. Then she heard her name again. It was closer, and it had a very familiar ring to it. She turned in her seat to see who owned the voice. There, walking toward her table, was Jake. She caught her breath. She had played around with the idea of seeing Jake while she was there, but never in a million years did she believe that she could be that lucky. Yet, there he was, coming closer with every second. She couldn't wait. She jumped from her seat and leaped into his arms. "Jake, is it you?" She held on for dear life. He smelled the same. He felt the same. It was like they had never separated.

Jake held onto her just as tightly, then pushed just far enough away to kiss her. Sarah felt like they had never been apart at all. They could have stayed there all day with their lips entangled but reality crept in. They remembered they were in the middle of a restaurant during lunch, and the place was crowded. He stepped back just enough to look at her from the bottom of her feet to the top of her head. It was Sarah. He had dreamed of holding her more than once since being at the University. "Sarah, I can't believe it's you. I've missed you so much."

Remembering where they were he asked, "What are you doing here?" Then looking at Samuel, he continued. "What are you doing here with him?" He wasn't jealous; it was Sarah after all, but he couldn't think of a reason the two would be having lunch together this far away from home.

He waited for an answer while battling the jealous virus. He wasn't sure, but he thought he saw Sarah's face flush slightly.

Was she guilty of something? No, he was allowing his mind to get the better of him. It was Sarah, and he knew that Sarah loved him, and only him. He settled his mind and deliberately held quiet and waited.

Sarah looked at Samuel and then at Jake. "It's a long story, Jake. You are not going to believe my summer and what is going on at home. Samuel and I are doing some work in the library today and got hungry, so here we are at the Olive Garden. I am so glad we decided to eat here because here you are. I couldn't have dreamed a better dream than this. It feels so good to see you; to talk with you."

Jake turned to Samuel. He tried hard to have an open-mind about Samuel and Sarah as he greeted Samuel. He held out his hand to shake Samuel's. "Good to see you, Samuel. We only met a couple of times before I left for the summer. It sounds like you and Sarah have been having quite a time back in Salyersville." Did he hear an edge in his voice or was it his imagination? Hopefully, Sarah hadn't noticed.

Sarah did notice. She had seen Jake get stiff and taut only a few times in their lives, but when he did it meant he was troubled by something that he didn't want to talk about to anyone. She usually could get it out of him, and they both felt better once he discussed it with her, but this time she wasn't so sure she wanted to discuss why he was so tense. She just wanted to be with him, to look at him, to enjoy their stolen time together.

Samuel watched as Sarah and Jake sent unspoken messages to each other with their eyes. His heart sank as he saw how they both adored each other. Maybe he thought he had a chance with Sarah, but now that he saw the two of them together, it was evident that he was the odd man out and couldn't have a place in Sarah's heart.

He had thought that the kisses they had shared might have meant as much to Sarah as they had meant to him. He thought he'd felt a connection to this girl that was more than just close friendship. Seeing the two of them together told him another story. He tried to conceal his disappointment, but he felt sure that Jake understood exactly how he was feeling.

He gripped Jake's hand and smiled a friendly smile. He tried to let down the cool, calm façade that was so easy for him to hide behind. He wanted to be friends with this boy. He was a part of Sarah's life, and he wasn't ready to give her up as his best friend. He wanted her to be more than a good friend, but if that was all he could have, then so be it.

"It's good to see you again, Jake. I think you have made Sarah's day. I have been working her hard over at the library, but now I see that the day of relentless work has been worth it even if we didn't have much success in our hunt for information."

Jake's face filled with bewilderment. "What have you two been looking for at the library? Why did you come to this library? Isn't the one at home open this summer?" He asked, knowing the answer. "You must be working on some really massive project." He laughed at his joke as only Jake could. Sarah had missed this about Jake so much. Her eyes danced as she watched the two boys talking. She liked the two so much, and she wanted nothing more than for the two to be good friends.

She turned to Samuel and was alarmed at the sad look on his face. Why was he so sad? Then she realized that Samuel was developing feelings for her just as she was developing feelings for him. They must not acknowledge this to each other or anyone else. She must protect her relationship with Jake.

She glanced over to Jake and saw his eyes moving from her to Samuel and then returning to her again. She dismissed Samuel and took control of the conversation, "Sit with us and have some lunch, Jake."

Jake, remembering that he was not alone in the restaurant, visibly collected himself and peered behind him to find his lunch companions. He motioned for two guys and three girls who were sitting across the room to come over. They all sauntered over. The boys noticeably sized Sarah up and down; no doubt they would be making comments to Jake later. Sarah felt uncomfortable with the attention.

Then her attention was torn from the boys to the girls who were walking toward the table. It didn't slip Sarah's attention that, counting Jake, there were three boys and three girls having lunch together. Now it was her turn to feel the wicked jealous monster. She eyed the girls with what must have been one of Samuel's cold pasted smiles. She greeted each girl with cheery hellos while listening for Jake to offer each girl's name. From far away she heard the names Tiffany, Joy, and Brittany form from Jake's mouth.

She didn't even like hearing him say their

names with the familiarity of old friends, or maybe even more, her suspicious mind told her. She scolded herself for even allowing herself to waste time thinking something as ludicrous as Jake cheating on her. After all, he found her first and seemed glad to see her, didn't he? She glanced over to Samuel to see him watching her closely. The fact that there were three girls with three boys hadn't been lost on Samuel either.

As she fought the rise of heat to her flushed face, Jake pulled her hand close to him. "I'm sorry Sarah, but I'm not supposed to see anyone from home until next week. I better go over with the others. We will have plenty of lunches in only one more week. Okay?" He looked concerned when he searched Sarah's face for a clue as to where she was emotionally.

He had known Sarah for a lifetime, and he was aware that Sarah's meeting the girls had not gone well. The others probably didn't notice anything, but he knew. He hated to have her stressed because of him. He wished he could tell her that things would be okay next week, but didn't know how without revealing his fears about their future. Jake had not cheated on Sarah, but he had gotten close to Tiffany during their work at the university hospital. He was scared that Sarah would notice. He never wanted to hurt Sarah.

Sarah didn't have time to feel hurt. "Well, I don't want to interfere with your lunch. Samuel and I are doing fine, and we will continue to be fine. Go ahead and have lunch with your friends, Jake." Her voice was laced with ice. Jake shrank back for just a moment and then gave her a quick hug and then he was gone. Sarah sat stunned. What had just happened? Was Jake there or were her hopes fueling her imagination? She looked across the table at Samuel. "Are we ready to go back to the library?" she asked.

By midafternoon, Sarah had forgotten or at least had successfully stopped the realization that Jake had new friends, and she wasn't a part of this in his life. While slumped over a document, Sarah heard Samuel loudly whisper her name from the end of the periodical stacks. "Sarah, are you in here?" He was searching the rows of books. Sarah had to giggle at his loud disruption in the silent library. She shushed him. When he got silent, she realized her giggle was loud and out of place there, too.

Samuel put his right index finger to his lips,

commanding her to be silent. She nodded and followed him out of the row of books and to the table he had claimed with the stack of work he had been perusing. He motioned for her to read the article lying in front of her. She picked up a newspaper page that he had pulled from the news section of the Herald-Leader. There was an article about a businessman who had moved to Kentucky. The article didn't click with Sarah. She wasn't sure what Samuel wanted her to see. "What am I looking at Samuel?"

She noticed that his face looked gray. He stared at her with a look of bewilderment. "This is my father, Sarah."

Sarah looked at the newspaper. On the front page was a large photograph of a man that looked amazingly like Samuel. The date was twenty years earlier. She stared at Samuel. "Your father lived in Kentucky twenty years ago?" She stared confused at Samuel. This newspaper is saying that your father lived in Kentucky twenty years ago? She stared at Samuel as if he could explain her confusion.

"Apparently, he did." He shook his head in disbelief. "Why did he live in Kentucky twenty years ago?" He looked at Sarah as if she could explain the newspaper article. "Maybe buying the farm on Buffalo Creek wasn't as random as I thought."

Sarah saw confusion and then hurt pass over Samuel's face. She wanted to make him feel better but didn't have a clue as to what she should say to him. She reached over the newspaper and squeezed his hand that gripped the newspaper.

Sarah's hand was enough to bring Samuel back to the present. "I read this article about a businessman who moved to Kentucky to lease the mineral rights from farms in small towns all over Kentucky."

"The man became news when some of the small communities complained about the strange happenings that occurred after he moved to the neighborhoods. It was the same story each time. He wanted a couple to move on the land to keep the façade of a farm going while he ripped out all of the natural resources from the ground. If any of the neighbors became suspicious, he tried scaring them or physically manipulating them with paranormal incidents to convince people that the spirit world was attacking them.

"This activity worked for months in several different small towns in southeastern Kentucky. Apparently, he left the state because one of his victims didn't scare so easily and reported him to the police. The article doesn't give the name or location of the victim. It says the victim requested to remain anonymous."

After Samuel finished Sarah looked puzzled. "Samuel, do you think your father is behind the happenings on Gamble Farm?" She searched his face for an answer.

Samuel's forehead wrinkled, evidence of his deep concentration. Could the happenings on Gamble Farm and the farms in the newspaper be connected? "I don't know if any of it connects, but think about it. Gamble Farm has been lying empty for ages. Not until someone buys it does suspicious occurrences begin. I mean, what are the odds of my father purchasing a farm in Kentucky, the same state where he had worked twenty years ago?" He shook his head. "I'm still wondering, why Gamble Farm?"

Sarah slowly sat down, attempting to connect the similarities of the happenings on Gamble Farm with the circumstances Samuel's dad had executed on the farming communities of Eastern Kentucky. The only difference was that they're located in the northern part of Kentucky. Still, the eastern section of the state is where natural resources are abundant. And, she and Samuel both had experienced similar violence to what is described in the article. Could this be what is happening at Gamble Farm?

She looked at Samuel and wrinkled her forehead. "So what do we do with this information, Samuel?"

Samuel folded the newspaper, so the picture of his father displayed on the front. "I guess I'll have to confront my father. I have no other choice. I'm sure we have found all we are going to find in here."

"Do you think he'll be honest with you Samuel? Will your father be truthful about his involvement with Gamble Farm?"

"I don't know, but I have to try to find out what his connection is to Gamble Farm." He took a deep breath and stated to himself more than to Sarah, "I'll try contacting him tonight. We won't be able to move forward until we know if my father is involved with Gamble Farm and the strange happenings there." Samuel took a long deep breath and stated, "I'm feeling good about this, Sarah. I think we've discovered something important today."

They left the library with a copy of the article in hand with information, but just as many questions, if not more, as they brought with them that morning. Samuel dismissed the worrisome facts he had discovered and directed his attention to the girl sitting beside him as he drove toward Salyersville.

Once they were on their way, the ride home was filled with music and laughter. They both felt as if a major clue to what was happening at Gamble Farm revealed itself to them. It was as if a huge weight lifted off their shoulders. Hopefully, the nightmare at Gamble Farm was about to end.

Sarah refused to bring up the fact that their evidence had Samuel's father in the middle of the incident. She was stunned to discover this bit of information so she was sure that Samuel must be in shock at the moment, as well.

By the time Samuel pulled into Sarah's driveway, the two had forgotten the seriousness of their situation and were just being teenagers. When Samuel parked and turned to face Sarah, she reached over and gave him a hug. Samuel pulled his arms around her waist and held on for longer than just a friendly hug. When he felt Sarah hesitating, he lifted her face to his, and he lightly kissed her. He knew he was overstepping, but he might not get another chance to show her how he felt about her. She allowed him to kiss her but then pulled away staring at him with tears in her eyes.

"Samuel, this can't happen. Jake and I are in love. We have been in love for many years. I'm sorry, but we can only be friends, and this can't happen again." She stared deeply into his sad eyes. She felt as if she was losing something near and dear to her.

Samuel nodded in agreement. He was buying time to regain his composure and when he began to speak he had to stop to clear his throat and start again. "I ... I know that, Sarah. I saw the two of you at lunch. I don't want to make your life difficult. I just want to remain your friend. I think the excitement of the day was intoxicating and we ---I ---got carried away. Please forgive me? I promise to keep my thoughts in friend mode." He held up his hand in Boy Scout fashion. They both laughed, and Sarah nodded her agreement.

As she jumped out of the car and made her way up the drive, she wondered if they could only be friends. They had kissed too many times for their relationship to be just friends.

Jake would be home in a few days, and things would get back to normal. Sarah would just have to control her urge to kiss Samuel. She couldn't help herself at times. She wanted to taste his beautiful lips and to feel his comfortable assurance that things would be okay. There was no denying that they had a strong connection.

She had seen Jake's face when he saw the two of them together today. How would she explain this if Jake asked? She wouldn't; what was there to explain. They had built a friendship over the summer. She felt her heart grow cold, just like Jake had become good friends with Tiffany, Brittany, and the others in his little study group. She was finding it hard not to be mad at Jake for dismissing her at lunch. She didn't care if they were not supposed to be seeing each other while he studied. What would have been different if he ate with her or with his new friends?

She made herself stop thinking like this. She would wait until Jake was home and they could discuss the summer with some distance from it and the events it had brought to them both.

Maybe she would talk to Cassie about what occurred at the restaurant today. Cassie would be neutral ground since she was friends with the both of them. That was what she would do; she'd call Cassie tonight and invite her over for a swim tomorrow.

Her thoughts drifted back to Samuel. She remembered his face when he realized his father was involved in a business in Kentucky twenty years ago. Not only was he involved in buying mineral rights from farmers, but the newspaper made it seem that he was conning the farmers. Sarah shook her head free of these thoughts. She couldn't do anything about the issue -- at least not tonight.

TWENTY-TWO

Sarah and Cassie lay on floats gliding through the water in the swimming pool when Sarah decided to approach the subject of Jake and his friends. "Cassie, I went with Samuel to Lexington yesterday. Guess who we saw at the Olive Garden?"

Cassie sat up on her float almost tipping over into the water. Once she got herself balanced, she pulled up her sunglasses to get a better look at Sarah's face.

"You went to Lexington with Samuel?" She waited for an explanation. Sarah squirmed under Cassie's piercing look. She didn't want to get on the subject of Samuel, but it was evident that she wasn't going to get that one past Cassie.

"We went to the University of Kentucky library to do some research on some issues he's having with his farm. Since I have been laid up here for the last week, he invited me to ride along, and I decided I needed to get out into the world away from here for the day, and I accepted." She studied Cassie and guiltily looked away.

"Don't look at me that way. It is not like that at all. We're friends, and he was trying to be a supportive friend--period." She stared Cassie down.

"Okay, I believe you. I know how much you and Jake care for each other so I'm not worried that you would do something stupid while he's gone." She slid a sideways glance at Sarah. "So, who did you see in Lexington?" She replaced her sunglasses on her face and relaxed back on her float.

Sarah hesitated, breathed deeply and jumped into the conversation. "Jake was there having lunch with some of his study partners." She waited for Cassie's reaction. She wasn't disappointed.

Cassie jerked up to a sitting position, and her float once again tilted, nearly tossing her into the water. Once she settled, she continued, "You saw Jake? That's great. How is he? Is he ready to get back home? Did you tell him how much we all miss him?"

She paused to breathe and then began again.

"Sarah, did you tell him what happened to you last week?" She stopped to give Sarah time to answer her last question.

Sarah was surprised at herself. She hadn't even thought about telling Jake about the incident. She stated to herself as much as to Cassie, "No, I didn't tell him. I honestly didn't think about telling him about it." She wondered at her own response.

Cassie stared at her friend. Sarah was getting nervous with the conversation. She sensed that something was adrift.

"Sarah, are you worried about something? What is up with you and Samuel? To be honest my friend, I'm a little shocked that you would travel four hours with a boy who isn't Jake. What did Jake say when he saw the two of you having lunch together?"

"He didn't say anything." Sarah felt the blood flow drain from her face. Was Cassie thinking she would cheat on Jake? Maybe he thought the same when he saw her with Samuel. But she reasoned he was eating with girls too. And, he didn't leave his new friends to eat with her either. She refused to feel guilty about having Samuel as a friend. Besides if everyone knew the whole situation she was sure that they would understand why she had gone with Samuel.

She answered, "Well, Jake wasn't alone either. He was dining with two boys and three other girls. Don't you think that is just a little convenient? I'm not saying he's cheating, but he was having lunch with girls; so why shouldn't I have lunch with Samuel?"

Cassie stared at Sarah. "I hope you two get together soon. This separation has cost you enough hardship." She splashed water toward Sarah's float. Sarah was trying hard to pull her mood out of the doldrums aimed a splash back at Cassie. Dodging the fountain of water, Cassie dipped into the pool head first. Sarah laughed so hard that she tipped over into the water too. Since they were wet, they swam a few laps and then found their floats again.

Sarah wanted to lighten the mood so she suggested, "Let's talk about something pleasant, shall we? Let's talk about the annual picnic this year. Jake will be home, and we can all be together--like an end of summer reunion."

"I'm looking forward to the celebration. Did you get to attend the one last summer? I can't remember. Josh had you so shielded to himself back then."

Cassie giggled. "Yes, I did get to come, but I didn't see a whole lot of people. The ones I saw didn't mean anything to me at the time. Josh and I kind of stayed by ourselves." She moved her feet in the water. "I'm looking forward to seeing everyone again too."

"Josh is already helping to build the platform for the dance floor. The Helton brothers are building the fence for the horse show next week." Cassie exclaimed, "I'm looking forward to all of the good food. The women of Buffalo Creek are the best cooks ever."

Sarah agreed. They began talking about the upcoming school year and slowly forgot the trouble that seemed to be waiting in the wings for Jake and Sarah. She was looking forward to having everyone back home and getting back to her routine. Summer had not been anything like she had imagined without Jake, but it had been hard. She would be glad when the paranormal fog lifted from the Gamble Farm and

Samuel could just be a kid like the rest of them.

She couldn't help but think of what life would be like once Jake came home, and she and Samuel were simply friends. No more playing at being boyfriend and girlfriend. She hoped the sparks that were flying between Samuel and her would stop once Jake was home. She wanted to include Samuel in their circle of friends. Samuel deserved to have them as friends for what he had done for them. Even if none of them would ever know what he went through to ensure their safety. She admired Samuel for his selflessness. She wasn't sure that anyone she knew would have been as brave and determined to stay on the farm with all the occurrences happening there.

Oh no, here she was again--thinking about Samuel. She looked over at Cassie as she rested on her float, "I can't wait to have Jake home." They both smiled and closed their eyes to dream of the year ahead of them.

TWENTY-THREE

Samuel paced up and down his living room staring at the phone as if it was evil. He knew he had to call his father, and getting him to listen to his son would be a miracle. Palmer Lazra was not a man with time for anyone. Samuel decided that procrastinating wasn't helping the situation. He gripped the phone and pushed his father's number. He realized he had not spoken to his father or mother since he got settled into his new home. Who leaves a seventeen-year-old boy to take care of himself without even checking on him? The Lazra's, that's whom.

Samuel tensed as he listened to the phone ring. Then he heard, "Hello, Palmer Lazra here."

Samuel cleared his throat trying to find his voice and after moments of static he replied, "Hello, Father. This is Samuel."

Samuel waited for a response but heard nothing.

He plowed ahead. "I'm calling because I have questions that I need to be answered."

He paused and waited again. This time, his father asked. "What's happening with the farm? Do I need to send my accountant down there? He can help you manage for a while."

Samuel laughed, "No, I don't need your accountant. I think the farm is doing well. I'm wondering if you had any contact with my farm before purchasing it this year."

There, it's out there. He knew he would have to dance fast to pin his father down for an answer. "Father, there has been unusual activity on the farm. I have been researching trying to understand what has been happening."

"What exactly do you mean when you say "unusual activity"? Be specific." Palmer Lazra demanded.

Samuel hesitated but not for long. He knew his father would dismiss him shortly. "There have been incidents in my home that I can't explain." He didn't want to be specific. He knew his father would dismiss him as a silly teenager. He knew his father well enough to know that confiding to him would serve no purpose other than derail the reason for his call.

Samuel cleared his throat, wanting to be strong when he approached his father with his questions, "I went to the University of Kentucky's library in search of any history the farm might have that would explain the happenings." Samuel rushed to finish his quest to find out if his father was involved with his farm. He knew Palmer Lazra would dismiss him shortly. "I didn't find any information on my farm specifically but in the process of searching I discovered newspaper articles about you in Kentucky twenty years ago. Is that correct Father?"

He waited for an answer. This time, he would wait out the silence. He needed his father to answer. He heard his father clear his throat and finally reply, "Yes, I did a few business transactions in Kentucky about twenty years ago. Why is this important to you and your little farm?"

Samuel avoided answering his father's question. "Father, I need to know if you had any attachments to Gamble Farm before purchasing it."

This time, his father answered quickly, "Absolutely not. I found that place through my friend John Flane." The silence was deafening.

"Do you want to get rid of the place already? I thought you would last longer than this out in the world."

Samuel responded with heat in his words. "I'm not ready to give up my home. I love living with the people in Salyersville. They have become my family."

Was he mistaken or was his father's voice cracking? "I understand, Samuel. You may stay on the farm. Is there anything else we need to discuss?"

Samuel smiled. He was doing it again. He was sliding past the issue and dismissing him. "Father, does the name Lykins mean anything to you?" The silence was deafening.

Samuel knew it was pointless but he would ask one more time, "Do you know of anything that might affect Gamble Farm?"

Palmer Lazra cleared his throat once again, "I don't know what you are talking about, Samuel. You are beginning to make me rethink allowing you to have that farm."

Samuel heard the threat in his words. "I'm fine, Father. Tell Mother I said hello. I love you both. Goodbye, Sir."

He hung up the phone with no answers, just frustration. He wondered why he thought he could get his father to answer him in any capacity. The idea was ridiculous. His parents had never cared enough to give him answers to any questions he'd had on any topic. They left that job to the school.

He would have to discover what connection, if any, his father had to this farm. It was obvious his father wasn't going to tell him anything. Was it because he didn't know of a connection or because he couldn't afford to "waste" time explaining things with Samuel? The thought that maybe his father was purposefully keeping something from him danced around in his mind. He shook his head as if to release this idea from his mind. Surely his father wasn't involved with the happenings on the farm. It was hard for Samuel to read his father.

He didn't have a clue from the phone call if his father had a connection with the farm or if, as Samuel had believed, Gamble Farm was just a small farm to keep Samuel out of their lives.

He would keep searching. Maybe the records office in Salyersville would have information that would lead him to answers about his father's connection with his farm and the Lykins family. At the least he could check out Mammy's story about the farm. He decided to go to the courthouse tomorrow afternoon and ask for their records for Gamble Farm labeled twenty years ago maybe farther back just to understand the history of his farm.

Whether his father was connected to the farm or not, Samuel knew that under all the farm's pleasant façade something dark lurked. He would face it himself, but he would not allow Sarah to be harmed.

He let out a deep breath and made his way to the barn to check on his horses. The workers were all around the barn spouting reports of progress to him as he walked around the farm. This was home. This was where he belonged. He had to discover what it was that threatened his home. Samuel smiled as he looked at the farm and the busy workers.

He was glad to hear that the fence was completed. Now, he needed to discover what was happening on his farm. Whatever it was, it could not take his home from him. He finally had people who treated him as if he mattered and he refused to give that up. He thought of Sarah and her family. This town was friendly and caring, and he was becoming a part of it.

TWENTY-FOUR

The next day Samuel left the farm and went straight to the courthouse. Marge, the lady in charge of the records, was waiting for him. Earlier in the day he'd called for an appointment and discovered this charming motherly woman on the other end of his call. Marge was more than happy to help him research the farm's history, especially if it was a summer project for school. Okay, he'd lied about it being a school project but what was he supposed to say? "Marge, I need to research my farm to find answers to why the entity that haunts it chose my farm." He smiled at the silliness of the truth.

None the less, Marge was there to help him search for answers to his questions. He loved this town. Never in his life had he had anyone dote on him like this elderly lady. A lady whom he had just met yet they'd formed an instant friendship. This is why he had to discover what was happening on his farm. He couldn't allow it to endanger these good people.

He was positive that something he had done in his work on the farm prompted the happenings. His good conscience wouldn't allow him to walk away to leave the people of Salyersville in danger. He would conquer this situation. He had to; there was no other alternative.

Marge had already stacked several long, thick books on a table in a side room adjoining the records library. "Okay, honey, here are all the files for the Gamble Farm since the 1800's. Good luck. Once you finish a book, you can stack it over here, and I'll put them up so you'll have room to work." She patted Samuel's shoulder and offered him an old office chair with rollers.

Samuel sat down causing the chair to squeak. He laughed at the sounds each movement made. How was he going to concentrate on work when the sound effects were hilarious? He looked at Marge, and she was holding in her giggles with her hand over her mouth. He looked helplessly at her.

"Let me get one of the chairs from the front for

you. This room isn't used very often. I'm afraid it has most of the discards from the office. You just wait, I'll have you as comfy as home in a jiff." Off she went in search of a chair for Samuel. Soon she was back with a chair and a sandwich. "Here's a little something we had left from lunch. You need some nourishment to think in here. There's a soda machine in the hallway." She replaced the squeaky chair with a comfortable one she had taken from the front office.

Samuel was touched by Marge's kindness. "Thank you, Marge. I appreciate all you are doing for me."

Marge smiled and patted the chair. "Come over here and get comfortable. Let's get you started on your work."

Samuel did as he was told. He took a large bite off his sandwich, looked at Marge, and smiled. Her face broke into a satisfied smile. "Now, if you need anything just give me a shout, and I'll be right here." And with that, she turned and made her way back to her office.

By the time Samuel was finished for the day he

and Marge were the best of friends. Samuel felt as if he had found a long-lost grandmother. Marge attended to him with the love and care that no one had ever shown him. Before he knew it, Marge had helped him organize his work area and vowed that she would make sure that no one bothered it until he returned.

The next day when he made his way to the courthouse, Marge was waiting with half of a red velvet cake and a fork. Samuel smiled, and before he realized what he was doing, he kissed Marge's cheek. "Thank you, Marge."

Marge blushed. "Oh my goodness. It's just a piece of cake. I hope you like it." She ushered Samuel into the record's room and set him up with a plate of cake and a large glass of milk. "Okay, you eat first, and I'll get your pile of books." Then she was gone, leaving Samuel to his cake.

After Samuel had finished two pieces of the cake and drank the glass of milk he wasn't sure he could get back to serious work. He knew he had to find something to help him keep his farm and to keep his new family safe. Even if most of these people were still strangers he felt as if they were his family.

He skimmed through page after page of records trying desperately to find something that would either dismiss his father or connect him to the Gamble Farm. He searched through every page of every book but found nothing that would answer his questions.

He decided to search the last name, Lykins. It didn't take him long to find proof of the events of the story Mammy had told them. There were death certificates filed for Samuel Lykins and Thomas Lykins on the same day. Both had the cause of death as gunshot wounds. Then, he found the death certificate for Henry. It to was listed as a gunshot wound. That was all the information he could find about the family.

After visiting the courthouse for three days, he bid Marge goodbye. He hugged his friend and thanked her for all her help and her food. "You're the grandma I've never had."

Marge hugged him with tears in her eyes. "Bless you, sweetie. You have to come back and visit me. Let me know when you are coming, and I'll be sure to bring you some of my cookin'."

Samuel grabbed his stomach. "That is a deal." He gave her one more hug and left the courthouse with a smile on his face. He felt a sense of peace and love.

As he left the town and headed toward Buffalo Creek, he felt the dread of going home wash over him. It made him angry to allow the old man that kind of power over him and his farm.

Samuel wondered if the old man would show himself again. It had been quiet since Sarah's incident. He didn't think for a moment that the old man had left. He kept watching and waiting. He parked near the house and stood out in front of the driveway studying the farmhouse as if searching for clues. His home looked peaceful. He murmured to himself, "How can the things that are happening in a place this peaceful be happening?"

He made his way through the house and entered through the kitchen. He smelled a delicious aroma. Too bad he had stuffed himself with Marge's homemade soup and cookies. He told the cook he would eat supper later and that he could go home. He was tired and would be retiring early this evening.

Once the cook left, the house was quiet. He hadn't lied. He was tired. He wanted nothing more than to find his bed and sleep. He turned off all the lights downstairs and headed upstairs to his room.

He had known it before he saw it. It felt as if an ice cube moved through him. It took his breath away. His skin felt frozen. He was frozen from the inside out. He tried to gain his composure as he stood halfway up the stairs, when from the corner of his eye he saw the stooped old man pressing in toward him. He was angry more than afraid at this point.

He turned to face the old man staring defiantly at his face. He didn't flinch as the old man pushed so close that Samuel felt he was taking his breath from his body. The old man breathed, "She is yours. Bring her home." Then he was gone.

It happened so quickly that Samuel wondered if he had been having a nightmare. He knew it wasn't a dream, and that scared him. He could face anything himself, but Sarah was in danger. He couldn't allow her to be in danger.

What was he going to do to keep this girl whom

he cared so much for safe?

He made his way to the comfortable modern bedroom he had made from the shell of a home left by the Lykins and Gamble families. He wondered if either of those families had experienced the old man as he had. He wondered what they had done in order to live their lives there. He slumped into his king size bed and wept for his farm and for the girl he wanted to protect.

TWENTY-FIVE

The next morning Samuel felt an urgency to find Sarah. He wanted to make sure she was okay. He knew that she would be at her mother's veterinary clinic. He walked to his car with alertness. He watched from the corner of his eyes trying to see if anything out of the ordinary was lurking. Nothing but the bright sun shining down on the horses and the surrounding woods.

He quickly made his way down the Buffalo Creek Road passing Sarah's house and then Jake's. The farms looked abandoned for the day. He knew that everyone was out and about this morning. He had heard about the picnic and he'd seen how everyone was busy getting ready for the big day.

Once he made his way to the clinic, he hesitated. What kind of reception would he get from Sarah? He dreaded bringing this new news to her, but he must warn her of the latest incident. He felt lost as to what to do about Sarah now that Jake was coming home, there would be no acting as if Sarah was his girlfriend.

Sarah was behind the desk. "Good morning, Samuel. How are you today?" Sarah noticed the dark circles under Samuel's eyes. She knew before he even said a word that this was not a good visit. "What has happened, Samuel? You look horrible."

Samuel smiled a weary smile. "That's what every man wants to hear from a beautiful girl." He cleared his throat and looked at the floor. "Sarah, can we talk for a minute?"

Sarah felt as if something had knocked the wind from her. Dread replaced the happy mood she had been in this morning. She frowned but obliged, "We can go into the files room. The clinic is slow today." She led him to the room she had spent most of her summer.

She turned to face him. "Please tell me this isn't what I think it is. I don't want to deal with this anymore."

Samuel raised his lowered head to look her in the eye, and Sarah knew the worst was yet to come. "What happened, Samuel?"

"He visited me again last night. He said that you are mine and that I must bring you home." He touched Sarah's arm, and she flinched.

"What are we going to do about this, Samuel? Why does this thing think I belong to you and that farm?" She began pacing back and forth forgetting that Samuel was there with her.

Samuel stepped in front of her to stop her pacing. "I won't allow anything to happen to you, Sarah. I promise I will do anything I can to protect you from this."

Sarah felt bile in her throat, "How can you protect me or any of the people in this community, Samuel? You look as if it has almost taken you out. I'm worried about you as well as for the rest of us."

Samuel dropped his head and talked to the floor. "I haven't found any history or connection to my family. I tried, but I've come up empty." He glanced at a pale-faced Sarah. "But, I do have a plan. I have been reading about other places with similar situations as mine and one thing that has helped is to have the home blessed and burn sage throughout to cleanse the house."

Sarah looked at Samuel's head. She bent down trying to see his face. "Do you believe that something like that will help?"

Samuel snapped his head up and regained his calm façade. "I think it's worth trying. After all, Jake will be home soon, and we need to have this settled before it becomes evident that you are Jake's girlfriend --- not mine."

Sarah nodded her head in agreement. "So, how do we go about getting this done?"

"I have contacted a lady from Lexington, who agreed to come to Gamble Farm to help investigate what is happening. She has done this sort of thing before, and she thinks she can help us." He looked at Sarah. She was visibly shaking.

"I'm going to meet her in town tomorrow. I'll bring her to the farm, and she will bless it. Afterward, I'll take her back to town, and hopefully, this will be over."

Samuel hesitated, "There is just one thing."

Sarah held her breath not wanting to hear what else he had to say. "What else could there be to this nightmare?"

Samuel stepped closer. "She said that since it is obsessed with you, that you need to be with us when we burn the sage and she blesses the farm." He watched Sarah.

Sarah fought the urge to scream. She felt her body go numb. Could she be brave enough to go back to Samuel's farm after what she had gone through there already? Did she have a choice? She knew she did not have a choice. She would do anything to protect those she loved. She just wanted her peaceful life back.

She straightened her shoulders and looked Samuel in the eye. "I will meet you in town and ride over with the two of you. That way I'll know what she says to do."

Samuel nodded. "I can pick you up from here at 12 o'clock tomorrow."

Sarah shook her head. "I'll meet you in town and ride over with the two of you." She turned and without another word led Samuel back to the waiting room of the clinic. "I'll see you tomorrow."

Samuel nodded in agreement and turned away. Sarah watched his slumped shoulders as he left the clinic. She felt her heart ache for this boy. He looked sad and defeated. She cared for him, but she couldn't jeopardize her relationship with Jake. She hoped all of this would be over tomorrow. She would introduce Samuel to some of the other kids in her class. Hopefully, they could be friends after this thing was finished and forgotten.

TWENTY-SIX

Samuel met Sarah at the Frozen Corner in Salyersville. He had arranged for Mrs. Lynette Simms to meet them at the family-run restaurant. Sarah watched Samuel as he tried to hide his anxiety. He was as nervous as she was which made her even more nervous. What if this didn't work? What did they do then?

She tried to act normally. She didn't want to draw attention to the two of them. She attempted to talk about the new school year beginning soon. She smiled and laughed but was sure that anyone with eyes could see that she was nervous about something.

Sarah chuckled. "Samuel, can you imagine what someone might think if they are looking at us right now? We look like we are ready to walk the plank or something."

Samuel smiled. "I guess you're right. We do look slightly uptight." He stretched the collar of his tee shirt from his neck.

As they began to release some of their tension a strange lady walked into the restaurant. She had a business suit on, and her hair was cut in a modern bob. Her eyes searched the restaurant. Sarah was confident that she was not from Salyersville and that she was searching for someone. No doubt she was looking for Samuel. Sarah cleared her throat, "Samuel, I think that lady might be Mrs. Lynette."

Samuel saw the woman and stood. He walked over to her and guided her back to their table. "Mrs. Lynette Simms, this is my friend I told you about, Sarah Arnett. Sarah, this is Mrs. Lynette Simms."

Sarah smiled at the attractive, older woman. She wasn't nothing that Sarah had imagined. She wasn't sure what she expected, but it wasn't this striking modernly dressed lady smiling at her.

"Hello, Sarah. I understand you have incidents with a spirit out your way."

Sarah blinked. She was direct and to the point. "Yes, we have had a few issues."

Lynette frowned, "If what Samuel tells me is true it has become more than a few issues. It sounds as if this spirit is obsessed with you. I'm glad you decided to join us today. It will help with the cleansing."

Lynette looked at the two teenagers. "When we do this we have to be direct, but not confrontational. You can't win a fight against one of these. We can request it to leave the home and leave the people alone to live their lives. This is what we will be requesting of this particular spirit."

She stopped talking as if waiting for the two to ask her to go on with her instructions. Finally, she finished, "Today we will tell this spirit that you want the home for yourselves and that it must move on. We will ask nicely but directly without giving room for it to stay. This will stop it for a while, but it may take more than one cleansing for it to leave the premises entirely.

Samuel and Sarah both nodded without comment. Finally, Samuel collected his wits and asked, "So, are we ready to go to the farm?"

Lynette stood. "I'm ready. Let's get this home

safe again." She followed Samuel and Sarah to Samuel's car. Sarah nervously got into the back seat and listened as Lynette gave detailed directions to Samuel and her on how to handle the cleansing.

TWENTY-SEVEN

Once in the house, Lynette removed white candles from her bag and placed them in different areas of the house. After lighting the candles, she handed Samuel and Sarah a bowl with a sage bundle. She lit the sage and instructed the two to tell the spirit exactly what they wanted.

Sarah felt her heart beating in her throat. She tried to hold the bowl of sage steady as she moved around the house asking the old man to leave Samuel's home and to leave the two of them alone so that they could be friends. Lynette had told them that their words were not as important as their hearts. She hoped the old man could see her heart.

She scanned the room until she saw Samuel roaming around the corners of the living room then up the stairs. She noticed his scowl as he mumbled words under his breath. He was so focused on his task that he didn't see Sarah as she moved through the living room near him.

She wasn't happy about being left in a room by herself, but she would be brave. She moved throughout the home speaking to the old man asking him to leave the farm and to allow her and Samuel to be friends.

After wandering in and out of the rooms, she found herself in the bedroom where she had been held captive. She felt strange about going back into the room where she'd been confined in for days, but she made herself enter. She refused to allow the door to close behind her. She kept her foot in the doorway until she could grab a tray from the chest and place it in the entrance to ensure that the door didn't shut.

Once she was certain that the door could not capture her in this gray room again, she entered. She scanned the room trying to recall the time she was left in here. She remembered bits and pieces, but couldn't remember large chunks of her time here. She shook her head in hopes of shedding the memory. She quickly made her request to the old man in the room then left. She couldn't help but take a glance back as she left and just for a moment she thought she saw the shadow of a man standing near the door. She quickly made her way back to the living room praying that Samuel and Lynette would be there.

Once in the living room, she tried to calm her shaking hands by setting the bowl of sage on a table and gripping its edge for stability. Just as she steadied herself, Samuel came into the room with Lynette. Sarah was never as glad to see anyone as she was to see Samuel and Lynette.

They didn't notice her state because they were in deep discussion about the entity of the house. When Samuel finally looked in Sarah's direction, he quickly realized that she was having a difficult time. "Sarah, are you okay?"

She quickly nodded her head, not wanting to allow the old man to scare her. She didn't want Samuel to feel that he had caused her discomfort as she knew he would if she told him what she had seen. She turned to face Lynette, "Do you think the cleansing has worked?"

Lynette, took a moment to look around the room and moved to distance herself from Samuel and Sarah.

Finally, she nodded. "I feel the room has lost the heaviness it had when I first entered."

Sarah refused to allow her mind to doubt that the cleansing worked. She had to believe that it would work and that they had seen the last of the old man. Once they finished cleansing the house, they walked the grounds around the house. They repeated the cleansing in the barns and around the fence.

Once they finished cleansing the grounds they quietly made their way to Samuel's car and left the property. When they had made their way out of Buffalo Creek and close to Salyersville Samuel questioned Lynette, "Is it okay for us to discuss what you found?"

Lynette nodded. "I think you will be okay. The entity was incredibly strong when we arrived. Once we finished and began to leave, I felt him very weakly. He was leaving or at least he will not be as dominating. You will not be in danger. If he doesn't completely disappear, we may have to do this again later.

Sarah breathed a sigh of relief. She prayed that the old man was gone, and Samuel could be comfortable in his home now. She prayed that Jake would make it home safely and that they could be good friends. She wanted the old man to leave, and they would never have to speak of the incidents of this summer again.

She looked at Samuel and was confused when she saw the look on his face. He looked as if he had lost something close to him instead of getting rid of the entity that haunted his home. What was he thinking? If this cleansing worked, it was a good ending to a bad situation.

Now they could look forward to school starting, to the end of summer picnic, to Jake and the rest of the gang coming home. Finally, things would be normal and calm again on Buffalo Creek.

Once they dropped Mrs. Lynette in town, Sarah turned to say her goodbyes to Samuel as she searched for the Rover in the parking lot near the Frozen Corner. Samuel moved close to Sarah. "Sarah, I am happy to be rid of the old man, but I will miss being close to you. I fear I have become quite fond of you this summer." He put his finger to Sarah's mouth, shushing her before she could say anything. "I'm well aware you are totally devoted to Jake. I will not try to come between the two of you, but I must tell you how much you have affected me. I hope we can remain friends, once this is over."

"Oh, Samuel, you know I consider you a close friend. I know you will become friends with the rest of our gang this year. I can't wait until the guys get to know you as well as I know you. You are a genuine Creeker now." She smiled but noticed the absence of joy she thought she would feel. She would miss this closeness too.

Without thinking, Sarah reached for Samuel's face and pulled him to her. He tenderly brushed her lips with his own as if testing her. She gave her lips eagerly, and he took them just as forcefully.

After a long lingering kiss, Sarah pulled away from Samuel and whispered, "Goodbye, Samuel. Our pretend relationship must end."

Samuel nodded. As he turned away to leave her, he saw the shadow lurking from the corner of his eye. It couldn't be what he thought. He was just paranoid now. He tried to laugh at himself but found his nerves shaking his insides.

Dismissing the unthinkable, he promised, "Sarah, I meant what I said about being your friend. I will be a loyal friend to you and Jake." He took one last look at the girl he had fallen for and walked away.

TWENTY-EIGHT

Jake's homecoming was exciting and nerve wrecking at the same time. The morning he was scheduled to return, Sarah leaped out of bed and began getting herself together. She wanted to look her best when he drove up the drive. She pulled on her new tee shirt and blue jean shorts. She took extra time to fix her hair and she knew her summer tan complemented her look. She finally felt ready to see her boyfriend.

She sat in the living room not wanting to miss the sound of his truck as he pulled into the drive. She waited for what seemed to be a very long time. After a couple of hours waiting, she gave up and wandered over to the barns to visit the cattle and horses. She could still hear Jake from the barns should he come while she was working. She would just have to be careful not to get her clothes dirty.

After she had finished working with the horses and there was still no Jake, she began to worry. What had happened to him? Surely, he had left long before now to come home, and yet he still wasn't here. She decided to call his house to check with his mom. Maybe he had been delayed, and the family had forgotten to tell her.

Jake's mom answered the phone. She was her cheery self. "Jake, honey, it's Sarah. Did you forget to tell her you're home?" Sarah's heart fell. Jake had gone home to visit his parents before coming to see her. Why would he do that? She fought back tears that threatened to spill.

"Hey, Sarah, it's so good to hear from you. I can't wait to see you." Sarah listened while squeezing the phone in her hand.

"I was concerned that something might have happened to you since you hadn't told me you had made it home. I'm sorry to bother you. Just making sure you are okay. I'll let you go back to your family." She hung up the phone without giving him a chance to speak. How could he treat her this way? Her Jake wouldn't think of treating her this way. Her Jake would have come barreling in the drive and racing up the walk just to hug and kiss her. Was this person still

Jake or had the summer changed him into someone else? She felt sad and angry at the same time.

She found the Rover keys and absently drove to her mom's clinic. Maybe she could help her with work to keep her mind off of Jake. As she pulled out of the drive, she passed Jake driving to her house. She whispered, "Now he shows himself." She waved and smiled and drove on down the road. She wanted to cry but kept her face frozen. She refused to allow him to make her cry.

She entered the clinic with a façade of cheer. "Hey, guys. I thought I'd come by for a visit since my days of being an honest-to-goodness worker are almost over." She bounced in and for a moment she forgot the bad day she was having. As the day progressed, her mood improved. She had so much to look forward to this year. She had gone through the whole summer without Jake and she had survived. If he was trying to tell her, he didn't want to be with her anymore then so be it. She would be fine. Life would go on without him. She tried very hard to believe the lies she was telling herself but failed miserably.

When her mom came in from the field, she saw

Sarah working in the back. She took the time to speak with her daughter before starting rounds with her patients.

"Sarah, why are you here? Why aren't you with Jake? You have been waiting for this day the entire summer, and you're spending it here with us and not him. I don't get it." She waited for Sarah's explanation. She refused to let it pass. Her daughter looked miserable, and she needed to know what was wrong.

Sarah had been through a rough time this summer. She didn't need to have more trouble in her life now. She sat down at the table where Sarah was working and waited.

Sarah knew her mother wouldn't leave until she spilled the whole story so she might as well get it over. "Jake didn't stop to see me when he came home. I got worried, and when I called his house to ask about him, he was already home. He hadn't even come to see me before going to see his parents. My Jake would never have put me on the bottom of his priorities." She heard her voice break. She refused to cry. She sucked in a deep breath and looked at her mother.

Joyce was in disbelief. "He didn't stop to see you?" She said it like she didn't believe Sarah when she said it. "There has to be an explanation. Did you allow him to explain what was going on? Have you discussed this with him, Sarah? What you are saying just doesn't sound like Jake."

Sarah had to admit that she hadn't given him a chance to explain. What possible explanation could there be for him to ignore her on his first day home? She felt worse than before now that someone, her mother no less, knew of the trouble they were having.

Joyce was confused. What had happened this summer that caused her daughter to become too close friends with the new stranger in town and the boyfriend she had adored her entire life to brush her off on his first day home? Things were not adding up, and she wasn't sure of what she could do to help Sarah. She looked at her daughter. Being an adult was hard, but this summer had been more than difficult. She wanted to hold her daughter in her arms and shield her from the world that kept hurting her.

But, she knew Sarah was strong and would make good decisions. The only thing she could do was to be there to support her daughter until she asked for her help.

She hugged Sarah and told her she would be ready to leave for home soon. She left her daughter to her thoughts and miseries for the moment.

Sarah waited until her mother was ready to go home before following her to Buffalo Creek. They got out of their cars, and as soon as she got to her front door, the Chevy truck pulled up behind the Rover. Jake got out of the truck and sauntered up the walk toward her. His face had a frown imprinted on it. Sarah tried to look natural, but couldn't hold back the tear that fell from her face. She looked closer and saw Jake had his own tears. He walked close to her and pulled her into his arms. "I'm sorry, Sarah. It was a stupid thing to do. I should have stopped first thing to see you."

She pulled away from Jake so that she could see his face. "Why did you treat me like that? You would never have treated me that way before you left. I don't like this about you." She stopped long enough for him to answer. At first, it was just silence then Jake allowed his breath to exhale heavily.

He stepped back and stuttered, "I know, and I'm sorry. I didn't know what to say. I mean, after the way we left each other the other day, I wasn't sure if you wanted to see me. I guess I was avoiding what has happened to the two of us while we've been separated." He paused, giving his words time to register with Sarah. "Please forgive me, Sarah?" He searched her face, but only found hurt and maybe a hint of anger.

"So what made you do that to me, Jake? You hurt me deeply. The one person in this world that I thought would never hurt me has hurt me to the core." She looked at him and when he didn't say anything she went on, "It didn't even occur to me that you wouldn't stop to see me before going on to your house. What has changed you, Jake?"

Jake looked at her with pain in his face. "Sarah, it isn't like you haven't changed. Do you know how it made me feel to see my girlfriend running around Lexington with a stranger? What were you thinking, Sarah; that I wouldn't see how he looked at you?" He shook his head and stepped back from her.

Sarah's eyes lit with fire. "Me, what was I

thinking? Unfortunately for you, you got caught with your little study buddies. How convenient for there to be three boys with three girls. And, then you had the nerve to dismiss me so you could go back to eat with your friends."

He stared at her. "Well, I could have broken the rules and risked my scholarship so that I could have had lunch with you and Romeo. How entertaining that would have been to watch you and Samuel sending google eyes at each other. I prefer not to watch another guy moving in on my girlfriend." He knew he was hurting Sarah, but she had hurt him when she showed up in Lexington with Samuel.

Sarah had heard enough. "I'm sorry you feel that way, Jake. I thought you knew me better than that. I guess we aren't what we claim to be, are we?" She looked at him with her accusing eyes, then opened the door and left him standing on the porch. She ran to her room, threw herself on her bed, and cried until she couldn't cry anymore. She didn't go down for dinner, and her mom and dad left her alone.

Later that night she heard her cell phone ring. She dreaded to see who it was. If Jake called and was mean again, she couldn't bear it. She looked and saw it was Samuel. Her heart felt lighter once she was positive that it wasn't Jake. "Hello," she answered.

"Sarah, good news; I had to call you as soon as I felt the lightness of the air at Gamble Farm. I haven't seen or heard anything since Lynette came to visit. I think we are safe from the old man now."

"Thanks, Samuel. I hope this will end this nightmare for you and us. I'm not sure that everyone is ready to believe that something paranormal was happening. Would you please tell me if anything else happens?"

"I'll call you. How are you, Sarah? You sound down." Sarah smiled at his concern.

"I'm fine, just feeling down." The last person that she wanted to know about Jake and her arguing was Samuel.

"Sarah, you know you can talk to me about anything."

"Thanks, Samuel. I know I can, but I don't have anything to say."

They hung up their phones, and Sarah noticed she was smiling for the first time since Jake came home. In only two days, the big end-of-summer celebration would happen at Jake's farm, and she would have to attend. He probably would have one of his UK girls with him. She would die of embarrassment if he did. No, Jake wouldn't do that to her.

TWENTY-NINE

The days lingered and still no word from Jake. The day of the celebration arrived, and Sarah was miserable. The last thing she wanted was to see all of their friends and let them know that she and Jake were not together anymore. But she had to face it before school started; might as well be now.

She dressed in her peach and teal sundress with tan sandals. She thought she looked pretty good to be in mourning. Instead of arriving with Jake, she went to the party with her mom and dad. They quickly found their friends, leaving her on her own.

She searched for Cassie until she saw Josh and Seth laughing near the dance floor. She made her way over and asked about Cassie. Josh took her hand and led her to the backyard. Cassie was sitting on a blanket waiting for Josh to join her.

"Sarah! I am so glad you found us. Sit. Isn't this fun? I wish we had these more than once a year." Josh gave her a quick kiss and offered to get the three of them some lemonade.

Sarah waited until Josh was out of hearing range and asked, "Have you seen Jake?"

Cassie shook her head, "No, I think he's hanging with Logan and Seth. Have you seen Isabelle? Is she still hanging with Seth? I hope they make it." Cassie realized what she had said about couples making it and froze. "I'm sorry, Sarah. You two have got to make it back together."

"I haven't seen Jake since the first day he came back, and that didn't go very well. I don't think he's interested in being with me." Sarah felt an overwhelming urge to move. "I think I'll walk around just to see what's happening at this shindig."

She stood up and put a bounce into her step leaving Cassie staring at her.

She hated the thought that others might feel

sorry for her. She hadn't asked about what Jake had been doing since coming home. She was sure Cassie knew what had happened between them. Josh and Jake were best friends. Sarah refused to look weak. She would leave the wondering to Jake. She hoped he wouldn't have that Tiffany girl with him today. That would be all that it took for her to break. She moved around the lawn and the barnyard talking with the different neighbors and her friends from school. She looked for Samuel but didn't see him anywhere. She thought for sure he would be here. Everyone was coming to this celebration.

As she turned the corner of the house to go back to sit with Cassie, she ran face to face with Jake. He smiled, and she smiled back. "I'm glad you came, Sarah."

She didn't know what to say. Was she supposed to stay away just because they were not boyfriend and girlfriend anymore? She felt her face grow cold, "Thank you."

She moved in a daze back to the quilt Cassie and Josh had brought. Cassie noticed the look on Sarah's face and made room for her next to the edge of the quilt. She wanted to shield Sarah from the hurt she was feeling. Why was Jake being such an ass?

Cassie had talked with Josh, but he was giving up nothing. He was trying not to take sides. He was, as was she, hoping that Jake and Sarah would get back together.

Sarah sat sipping her lemonade and thinking. She wished she had found something else to do today instead of living through this pain at Jake's house. She was sure there was something she could be doing at the clinic. She had made up her mind to tell her parents she wanted to leave to visit Homer, a horse that was at the clinic when she saw Samuel strolling through the crowd. He stopped to talk with different groups of people. Sarah noticed his cold façade and smiled. He hated this as much as she did. Maybe she could get a ride with him to the clinic. But, if she left the party with Samuel, Jake would be even angrier.

"Samuel, would you mind driving me to the hospital? I need to see the horse I was concerned about yesterday." She refused to allow her mind to tell her what a disaster she was heading for doing this in front of Jake. He had made her life miserable, and so be it;

she was tired of playing his game. She impatiently waited for Samuel to respond to her request.

Samuel knew from the moment that he saw her that she was upset. He didn't know what had gotten her in this mood, but he didn't want to add to the problem. He thought this might be because Jake was staying away from the gang like the plague and Sarah was pretending not to see him drifting from group to group.

He wanted Sarah, but not like this. "I'm going to get myself a glass of lemonade first. Would you like a drink for the road?" He looked at her face with a smile that told her that she was okay, and he had her back. She smiled back. He watched her visibly relax as the muscles in her face smoothed out and her hands stopped clenching the blanket where she sat.

He turned and walked toward the lemonade table while searching the crowd for Jake. He was halfway across the lawn when he spotted Jake near the front porch of the house. He made his way over to him. "Excuse me, Jake, but do you think we could talk?" He politely waited for Jake to respond.

Jake lifted his head, and Samuel saw the dislike or maybe jealousy that lay just under the surface. Jake motioned for Samuel to follow him inside the house. Samuel followed. He didn't know what to expect, but he had to do this for his friend.

Once they were in the house, Samuel didn't hesitate, "Jake, Sarah has never been anything except a friend to me. We have had things happen this summer that pushed us together. When Sarah was attacked; I felt responsible."

Jake straightened at the mention of the attack. "What are you talking about, Samuel? Sarah was attacked? When? By whom?" He was inching closer and closer to Samuel. He needed to know. What had happened and why had no one told him?

"You mean no one told you about Sarah's attack?" Samuel was confused. Why wouldn't Sarah tell him about her experience? Surely, she would tell her boyfriend about an experience that was such an emotional strain on her. "Jake, Sarah hasn't told you about the attack in the woods between our farms?" Samuel's face mirrored Jake's confusion.

Jake answered more to himself than to Samuel. "No, we haven't been talking a lot since I've been home." He frowned. Why had he been such an ass? Samuel had been here this summer to help Sarah after she was attacked -- something he would have done if he had been home. Sarah didn't deserve this treatment from him.

"Samuel, please tell me what you know. I feel I've done Sarah wrong, and she probably won't tell me herself."

"No, I won't tell you. That is something that you need to hear from Sarah.

You need to talk with her. I want you to know that Sarah and I are only friends." Samuel allowed Jake to see his real face. The emotions he felt were evident in his eyes. "I also want you to know that I care for her very much. If the two of you are over then, I will try to win her affection. You need to decide where you stand with her.

"Until the time that you two settle your relationship, I will remain the good friend. If the two of you are still in love with each other, I will continue to be the good friend, and I hope to be a good friend of yours. I just don't want to see Sarah in such a state as she is in today. Will you take care of it, like--right now?" His eyes were demanding and bordered anger.

Jake didn't know whether to be angry at this person standing in front of him or to thank him for offering his friendship instead of trying to steal Sarah's heart. Samuel had done what any good friend would do. Sarah didn't deserve the treatment Jake was giving her. His actions since he had been back were inexcusable. The truth was that Jake did want to be with Sarah, yet he didn't want her to stay with him just because they had always been together. He wanted her to decide with her heart.

"Thank you, Samuel. I appreciate your candor, and I'll work things out with Sarah as soon as I can find her." Jake turned to leave and then turned back to face Samuel, "You are truly a gentleman -- not many would tell their rival of their intentions."

Samuel nodded. "I only want what Sarah wants. She's been a real friend, and I will protect her feelings if I possibly can." He smiled at Jake, "Even if her happiness means she wants you instead of me."

Jake nodded, "We seem to be on the same page, friend. Shall we allow the lady to decide which of us she wants? Now, I need to find out what happened to my best friend while I was away." He turned and was gone.

Samuel's smile was lost on Jake. He wasn't sure why he smiled. He guessed he was happy that Sarah would be happy. He didn't know how he would contain his feelings for her but he would – he must. As the sadness settled over him, he noticed someone standing in the foyer of the Arnett Home. He turned to face the old man with the full head of white hair and gold-rimmed glasses. Samuel gasped. "How did you get here? I thought you were gone. Please don't hurt my friends. Please go home and I'll return to you. Just leave them alone."

The old man stood still as if waiting for Samuel to react to him. While staring at the old man, Samuel's anxious face became calm and serene. He stepped toward the old man and calmly asked: "Shall we wait for Sarah or go find her, Sir?"

Jake found the waiting Sarah. He sat down beside her on the quilt. Cassie and Josh discreetly left the quilt and began socializing with the small groups of people that congregated throughout the yard.

"Sarah, I am so sorry for how I have acted toward you since I have been home. Please forgive me. I have no excuse for my actions other than my foolish jealousy. Samuel and I have been talking. He is a good friend to you, and I am sorry I have been the jealous boyfriend. Will you forgive me?"

Sarah reached up to caress Jake's frowning forehead. "I guess I have to forgive you. I've been having the same feelings about your friends, Tiffany, and company." She smiled at her long-time love, and he answered her with a kiss that had been a long time coming. She missed this boy, and she wanted nothing else other than to be in his arms.

As they kissed and the sun shined down on their cozy quilt, Samuel, and the old man stood looking out the window at the couple. The old man raised his hand to Samuel's shoulder and gave him a nudge.

Josh and Cassie came into the living room laughing. "Samuel, I didn't know anyone was inside the house." Josh quizzed.

Samuel turned from the window, "Jake and I needed a little privacy to discuss a few things."

Cassie frowned, "Is everything okay?"

Samuel turned and motioned out the window. "Take a look. I think everything is going to be just fine." He smiled and for an instant, Josh thought he saw the shadow of the old man that Samuel would someday become. It was eerie to see Samuel like this. He reached for Cassie's hand. The air in the house was cold, and Samuel had replaced his smile with his usual cool façade.

ABOUT THE AUTHOR

Vivian Ward Crump is the author of two novels: *Lingering Soul of the House* and *Stranger Neighbor.* She is working on the third book of the *Lingering* Trilogy.

Vivian worked as a writing consultant for her hometown of Salyersville for several years. Once she relocated to Shelbyville, Kentucky she taught language arts and writing to sixth, seventh, and eighth grade middle school students.

When Vivian retired from the classroom she became serious about her passion for writing. It was then that she began her journey of publishing novels that were sitting on shelves waiting for her to be ready to share.

Vivian lives in Shelbyville, Kentucky with her family and until recently, her dog and best friend, Shelby. Unfortunately, Shelby passed away this year and her spot next to Vivian's writing desk is empty.

Vivian spends a lot of her time visiting her mother who still lives in her hometown of Salyersville, the setting for the Lingering trilogy. Her favorite times are spent with friends and family.